Gone to Pieces

Gone to Pieces

BENJAMIN FIDLER

WINNER OF THE 44TH ANNUAL 3-DAY NOVEL CONTEST

anvil
PRESS

ANVIL PRESS | VANCOUVER | 2023

Library and Archives Canada Cataloguing in Publication

Title: Gone to pieces / Benjamin Fidler.
Names: Fidler, Benjamin, author.
Description: "Winner of the 44th Annual 3-Day Novel Contest".
Identifiers: Canadiana 20230450717 | ISBN 9781772142174 (softcover)
Subjects: LCGFT: Novels.
Classification: LCC PS3606.I36 G66 2023 | DDC 813/.6—dc23

Book design: Derek von Essen
Represented in Canada by Publishers Group Canada
Distributed by Raincoast Books

The publisher gratefully acknowledges the financial assistance of the Canada Council for the Arts, the Government of Canada, and the Province of British Columbia through the B.C. Arts Council and the Book Publishing Tax Credit.

Anvil Press Publishers Inc.
P.O. Box 3008, Station Terminal
Vancouver, B.C. V6B 3X5
www.anvilpress.com

PRINTED AND BOUND IN CANADA.

"A greenish sun in the pale blue sky shone like an unripe apple. Since the thaw had set in, the ice bound surface of Lake Ladoga had begun creaking; it wailed, at times it shrieked shrilly as if in pain. In the deep of night, from the end of the korsu we could hear it suddenly crying out, wailing for hours at a time, until the dawn … A green vein cut across the horizon, it seemed at times as if it could be seen throbbing, as if it were full of hot blood.

   That morning we went to see the icebound horses being freed."

— Curzio Malaparte, *Kaputt*

The Horses

My father's life was a single story.
I hated that story.

Every morning my father took his coffee the same way. Every evening it was the same pipe in the same chair, the same television station. He took to the news of far-off wars and riots in the streets the same way. There was a world he wanted but he could not find it through the black and white newsreels that filtered down to him in the evenings. He ate our mother's meals with the same fork. The same knife. He drove his car to work the same route. He balled his fists in anger the same way. The cadence of his voice never varied, never once changed direction as he would curse my mother, strike her, walk away. These habits became his soul, but isn't that all a soul is anyway? The things we do over and over again? They wound around him like layered valances. They hummed with electricity but did not move from their course. Everything wants to move, everything wants to change course, but my father — too set in his ways or too frightened of what a different direction might hold — did not allow that change. Refused it. He became the ice horses of Lake Ladoga. He wanted something in his life to freeze in an instant and live out longer than he could ever hope. He was a creature seeking some self-same thing. He was a creature of habits. He wanted that same thing we all want — eternity.

We all form habits. Some of us embrace them. Others think they can change, think they don't become some peasant plowing the same long furrow over and over again, turning earth into earth, but we all do. We all put that sharepoint deep into the earth.

Before I stood on the ledge above the lake, no two places could be within me at the same time. I drink the same coffee, but never in the same place. I drive the same car but never the same roads. I don't allow myself to live the sameness over and over again. I'm one but never both. When you see it, it haunts you. It takes the very idea of the world away. Isn't it enough the earth takes the same path year after year around the sun? Spins the same direction every day? The moon spins at the same rate and in the same course as it always has? Isn't it enough not being more?

I don't have an answer to these questions, but neither did my father. He was some obtuse figure, some statue in the distance, cracked and weathered, the silhouette of a sculpture putting chisel to stone.

I guess this is why I hated the story. It was always the same, always the same words, the same lake, the same horses. The same frozen moment in time. I know this is what a story is, but with each retelling I hoped some small detail would change, some horse might make it through the flames and through the ice and out the other side. But one never did. In the end everything ends.

This was before our mother died. After her death, my father grew quiet and the story slowly disappeared. It melted away from the hole of where she used to be. It was the first time in his world in which the habits broke. It had become so routine, so expected that on those rare occasions when a guest would break the threshold of our house it would play in my mind like a ghost recording. I pictured our guests as lost souls wandering the dry desert of the world looking for an oasis but in their seeking finding only the broken well that was our family.

He did what he could to hold the ritual of habit. My father still drank the same, still moved in the same way about the house. He clung tight to the world of his past. The news had changed but his contempt for the world hadn't. The food, now prepared by a nurse or a neighbour or the frozen section of the grocery store had changed, but the fork and knife had not. Toward the end he could not drive — or so I was told — so every morning he would ask his nurse to drive him along the same route to work he had done for those three dozen years. He needed to know the slaughter would continue. This was part of the story.

He needed to make room for a ghost. Whose ghost I don't know. Maybe my mother's. Maybe his own. Hidden inside him was contempt for himself, for his frail and failing body. Maybe he wanted to be a ghost himself because ghosts can live without time. Maybe it was the path he could take to see, one final time, the ice horses. He felt lost in his human form. He was not a man but a beast. There was a time when my brother and I would watch him transform into a spectre right before our eyes. Become something else besides what we thought we knew. To us, and to my mother, we envisioned his end. But he couldn't see that. He thought himself a man and a man of the world at that, the bringer of things civil and wonderful to the light. The creator of culture. The harbinger of war. Maybe he saw himself then as a ghost in the world of the physical and real, a spectre wandering the lost story of the ice horses of Lake Ladoga carrying each word like a lit torch into the dark.

So I guess this is a ghost story. It's a story about horses and ghosts. It's a story about horses and ghosts and whatever space is left to survive between the two.

Before he was a ghost, my father was a butcher. He worked in the part of Chicago that smelled the most of offal, of raw flesh burning and blood drying. When we lay dying on the bed on the westside, I took the el to midtown and walked a bridge over the river looking for the only smell I remembered of that place. When I found it, it stung. It was the inside of something long dead. It was a clouded night when the sky was pulled close over my bedroom window. I heard again the bellow of the cattle, the soft squeals of the hogs stuffed in their holding pens. My brother and I would sing the words they spoke to one another. Make stories of their past. They were born in the sunflower fields of Kansas. In their first waking moment they looked up to see the spinning heads of the sunflowers, following the sun in its arc across the sky. They watched as the season drew long and cold and the once yellow centre of the flower heads turned black and the seeds not pecked clean by the migrating finches fell to the earth.

When I was ten I spent a day with my father among the carcasses. While he was on the floor I drew the same stale landscape over and over again on a stack of paper with the blue and black pens my father had given me from the office of someone who didn't spend their day with a knife. I drew a field of sunflowers. After lunch he took me through the pivot doors — tacky with what makes up a body — onto the cutting floor.

The hogs lined the wall like laundered shirts hanging from thick steel hangers. They were split down the centre and I could see their slow decay as I looked down the room. As if somehow moving down the track could make a body disappear. It was cold and my fingers froze. I rubbed them together. My father took them and pressed them into his as if in prayer. He rubbed his hands over mine. I could feel his calluses, the places deep with the memory of the knives he held. They left an oily greasy smell on my hands. That same smell he brought home with him each night. The same smell he worked to replace with liquor each night. The same smell of habit.

He led me to the place he stood all day and lifted me to see one of the carcasses hanging from the ceiling. I could see the red and white of the muscles swirl around one another, the tips of bones, their absolute white, freed from the hold of tendons and ligaments, bent opposite of what they once were. Angles of an afterlife.

"You see this," he said and drew a line with his hand over the top of the hog's shoulder. "This is my cut." I stared at the imprint he left in the air waiting for the meat to fall from the bone but it didn't. What some people study for years in dissection rooms and high walled ivory towers naming at once every movement of the body in Latin, my father studied on the bloodied floor of the abattoir. He knew the body through its parts. Shoulder, hock, trotter. The butt of the hog — section of marbled shoulder meat once stored in small wooden casks. Chops, the names of the thing, the action which made it one. He gave us these same names. He pushed my shoulder, "the picnic" he would say. Grabbing tight my shin, "the shank."

The whistle blew. The butchers returned from lunch. The smell of stale tobacco masked the smell of blood.

"Let's get you back to the other side," he said.

The phenomenon my father talked about is called supercooling. I found this out years later from a boyfriend.

"He's not entirely wrong you know," he said to me after I had recounted the story to him as best as I remembered.

"Not wrong?" I said. "The story is pure fiction."

Jack passed the joint to me and pulled the sheet up below his armpits and tucked the edge of it under his thigh. This was his habit.

"Listen, all I'm saying is there is some truth in the physical properties of water that could allow for such an event." We listened to Vic Bondi sing about his destiny from the tin speakers of a clock radio.

I took a drag of the joint and let the smoke slowly escape my mouth and I watched it swirl in the still air of the room. Jack was an aspiring physicist who lived uptown near the university. We had meet at an Articles of Faith show on the upper east side, he was the only other person in the room without glue or colour in their hair and as much as I wanted to be a rebel, as much as I wanted to find the person with the most metal embedded in their face and the tallest spikes on their head to parade around the house to piss off my father, I found myself with Jack by the end of the night.

Jack was a second-year PhD studying the particle mechanics of neutrinos or something along those lines. He was six years older than me.

"It's called supercooling," he said.

"Supercooling? I said, as if he were making up this whole thing.

"Water freezes at thirty-two, right? But it needs something to freeze against, something to start the reaction. It needs a seed." Jack pinched his thumb and forefinger together and stared at it as if he had caught the thing that ice needed right there in that second story studio apartment on the lower southside.

I took another drag and passed him the joint. "Here's your seed."

Jack took the joint. He tilted his head back and blew three concentric rings in the air. I thought I could see the music vibrate through them.

"All I'm saying is he's not making the entire thing up. You should give him at least that much credit."

Jack was about all I had then, him and a shitty job waiting tables during the morning shift at a twenty-four-hour diner that required me to arrive early but not sober. I was nineteen and had left the house three years earlier and spent the better half of my sixteenth year moving from friend's couch to friend's couch until their parents became concerned and asked the question that inevitably led me to pack up and leave — "How are things at home, Curzi?"

It was the summer of '86 and when my father had started in once again with his story and when he had once again finished in the same way he always did I asked if he thought Reagan might do the same to the horses of Grenada or Panama. I forget now which conflict we were in but I knew my father supported them all. He had voted for Reagan, first in '80 because that "softy" Carter couldn't get our people out of Iran and then again in '84 because habits are hard to break. I knew any mention of Reagan and my dislike for him would instantly start my father.

"Honey, let's not talk politics now," my mother said, but I asked again and my father swirled the last bit of ice in his glass before taking it down.

"Well?" I prodded.

"Curzi, stop," my mother said. I ignored her and stared at my father.

"No, fuck that. Fuck your horses. Fuck you," I said. It was pointed, sharp as a needle. So sharp it stung me too.

"No, it's fine, mama," my father said. "She can speak." He paused, then as if he were ending the story of us said, "You should know then, after all these years, about pack animals. If it is me you are angry with fine. But the horses have nothing to do with it, after all, we have them because of people like you." He looked me square in the eyes. My face was swelling with tears. I could feel their hot tracks running down my cheeks. "Some people in this world carry the burden, and some people need the burden carried for them."

I left a few days later.

I have no doubt that my father lived a single story because he came from a place that didn't have one. When he was born the story had been erased, remolded, burnt under the incendiary bombs that were dropped on his world.

He was born in the last year of the war into a broken Italy, crumbling, torn apart. His father and mother immigrated to America. His father, a farmer from the countryside south of Rome, had aided the allies in the war and had secured a pass to the new country. They settled in Chicago, the trip hurried in hopes that my father would be born on American soil. The day after they reached Chicago, in a room rented from a friend from a friend from the old country, my father was born. So quickly, so silently, they thought he was dead, a curse brought from the old country. The curse of death. Before he turned a year, his parents were dead inside the steel hull of an American made car.

He never talked about what happened in his early life and I don't know much if he remembered himself. I know there were scars where there shouldn't be. I know he moved as much as the Romans legions did, from place to place, town to town, in search of conquest, in search of rest. He became taken with the dream of an Italian empire after reading the works of Gentile and Mussolini. He talked incessantly about restoring the past. He found *Kaputt*, a book by Curzio Malaparte about the eastern front. It was how he found the story of the ice horses.

The day he turned eighteen he changed his name, from a name no one knew — because he told no one — to Antonio Malaparte. He found in his new name the past he never had. He found the chaos of his history and he loved it. My brother was named Candido and when I came next, he named me Curzio. My father would parade me through the shops of Chicago's little Italy neighbourhood. He would buy thick-sliced ham from the delis and small raspberry thumb cookies from Lena's bakery, the second building in from the bank. In me he had born not a daughter but a revolution; with me he had a new home built from the ruins of his incarnate past. I became the child of a war-torn country's dreams. The name held captive every grandparent, every disaffected expatriate of the old country and they each opened up to me with the stories of their past. I became a canvas and they painted on me what they hoped would have been their life. I grew tomatoes and flowers from pots on the terracotta balconies framed by the pure blue sky and the green of the sea. I was the breeze that swept through their house and blew the soft linen curtains into the alley washing the smell of cured fish and ripe olives from house to house. I carried all of their stories and I carried his. I took what I was given, it was written on me and I became the story.

"Ah, Curzio," someone would say, "the blessed."

And my father, carving a small cross in the air, would agree. "Yes, yes, daughter of the ice horses."

For years I thought my father had named me Curzio as a prompt for him, a pedestal for his rants and speeches. I was a child puppet and he was the puppeteer. He told me as we walked Taylor Street that Curzio was a name to be proud of and would launch into a speech about the history of the name, the pride that came with it.

"It means to be enlightened, intelligent. The name gives you the power to shape the future because you are named for what has yet to come."

I have taken for all these years my father's word, maybe the only words of his I have taken to be true, about the meaning of my name. And when people ask what my name means I tell them these same words.

I once asked my father why he never took the name Curzio for himself. He did, after all, have the chance to be whoever he wanted to be when he took his new name.

"I did not take the name because it was not right in the order of the world to take the whole name. A person spends their life building themselves. They may live with a name their whole life but it is only with their death that the name has meaning, has purpose. It becomes of them something solidified, frozen in time. What is a person when they are born? Nothing. They are nothing. Bones and flesh and blood but nothing. They are a corpse, not a ghost. It is only when they die that they become something, that their imprints on this world become who they were. People say, 'Oh that was Caesar. He was Caesar because he lived the life of Caesar.' I could not be Curzio. I had not lived my first life as such. I could only be half the name for I was half done living.

"You see, I gave you the name Curzio because you were born a Malaparte and you could take the name and do with it what you wanted. You could become the name again."

When I asked him why he didn't give it to my brother — give a boy's name to a boy — he said "That is nonsense. A name is a name. You make with it what you make with it. Your brother was not Curzio. You were."

And so maybe this is why I would linger at the table with my father as he told the story of the ice horses. Maybe I felt some responsibility to the name, to him. As much as I grew to hate it, as much as I grew to resent the entire world that my father had built in that single story, I felt some pulling toward having to hear it through each and every time. I had to wade through the story just as he wanted.

And so, he would start the story, "Can water make its own history? Can a horse do the same?"

At one time Lake Ladoga was a sea, part of the great expanse that was the Baltic Sea, the sea the Vikings and Norse people of prehistory traced with their long boats. But in 1942 it was a lake, a lake separated by a narrow isthmus from its former self, a thin strip of land and the city of Leningrad all that stood between it and returning once again to its former salty self. As winter approached, the siege of Leningrad grew more intense, the Finnish forces pushed with little resistance toward the heart of the city. Men lay wounded and starving all the fall before. The Russians were suffering. Children wasted to outlines of skeletons. It was better to drown in the sea than starve on bread made of wood pulp.

The siege brought acts of immorality no parent would, in a thousand years over, ever want to think about. To kill a child, to save it from the actual hell of the world, or to push ahead into an unknown?

The Finnish vanguard had pushed through the wilderness of Vouksi and Raikkola with ease as if part of them were part of the wildness. The moved in herds like reindeer. The Russian supplies were slow in coming. The tugs and small boats stocked with ammunition and food were held up in some long off place. The Russian soldiers retreated in self-preservation. They ate bark. They ate dirt. I cannot say with certainty that in times of great need they did not once think about the taste of the flesh of the man who lay dying next to them. It was October and winter was already upon the near arctic places. One night, a cold settled over the Raikkola, a cold of the deep arctic, that does not surround but penetrates all things it touches, like a wave. It was a cold nothing could survive. The native tribes of the north have many names for it but they all mean the same thing: death.

The men, near froze to death in their hiding, were surrounded by exploding shells. The trees splintered into giant toothpicks; their canopies shredded into pulp. The artillery fire ignited the dry needles of late autumn, Fire roared through the wilderness down through the isthmus. The soviets were surrounded by fire and water and the horses bellowed as sparks and embers caught in their manes and settled on their backs. They tore through the wall of fire and rushed to the edge of Lake Ladoga. Thousands of horses shot into the water, hoofing their way over one another in a mass of tangled limbs and bays and wild eyes reflecting the flames. They pawed over one another, deeper into the cold lake. And then, like a crack travelling through crystal, the water stopped moving and froze in a flash, expanded into blocks. The sound of ice cracking tore through the wilderness, the bays of the beasts echoed off their icy tombs. Waves froze solid in their rise, remaining kinetic in their shape, static in their form and the horses began to turn back toward the shore but could not for they could not swim. Their bodies locked into the ice, the last screams choked from their body as they ceased their movement. The lake froze solid in an instant, a chain reaction triggered by the violent convulsions of war. Burn or freeze or die, they were all three the same that night. The lake frozen, the air still arctic, the heads of the horses suspended in the void.

This is the story my father told, slowly, methodically, each time adding some note of biblical reference, some undertone of apocalypse. It grew into a boated and rotted corpse like the horses the next spring.

My mother — how she had the patience I do not know — would sit quietly, expressionless, lost among the eyes of the room. I don't know how she felt about it. It was not something we talked about. The story only appeared in the shadow of company, late in the evenings after wine and liquors and food and what was, until that point, buoyant words and gentle conversation. Why suddenly, and without provocation my father would tell this story none of us knew. Why he blew across that table like the arctic winds we didn't understand. It was as if he were under some contractual obligation to do so, some contractual obligation written in some unseen ledger regarding the magical curiosities of this world and it was only he who could pass down these wonders to the rest of humanity.

The first time I heard this story I did not understand the base figure of its world. I did not know what war was or how it was used. I did not understand the physics of ice or its formation. I knew only that ice was water and water was ice. One solid. One liquid.

One could become the other. Each the same substance just a different form. I did not know the way the world is bent on carving itself up, obsessed with imaginary boundaries set about to stir pride or resentment among people. I did not know of any of this the first time I heard the story. I did not know any of this the last time I heard this story from my father. But that was the point of the story, or so I guess all these years later. To make real the parts of the world we might never see. To hold in place the terribleness that hangs in the air like the cold of an arctic night. To build through the repetitive motions of life a history all your own.

I saw our horse for the first and only time in 1978. It was one of my father's few days off and he pulled me from school, called in some unnecessary excuse for my absence.

"It is equine in nature," he told the school.

He packed us lunches of salami sandwiches, apples and cans of soda — we never drank soda. We left early in the morning. I fell in and out of sleep to the talk radio. My father was manic, excitable. He had spent the better half of the year on the phone late into the night and early in the morning, pacing in the kitchen talking loudly in slow English to some distant place. He might have walked out the door and disappeared down the road were it not for the beige curled cord that kept him grounded in that room. Money disappeared. Time stopped. He was after something which had fled but was returning.

I could smell the lake. We were on our way to see what he had bought through those long-distance, late-night calls.

I woke to a gunmetal sky. Low clouds hugged the shore and white smoke billowed from the stacks stood like fence posts on the thin shore. The Buick rocked slowly over the pavement; the hum of the tires whorled in the cab. I half-dreamed of the horses and the ice. The story in my eight-year-old head was a fairytale and I held onto the idea that somehow the horses, once thawed, would trot out of the water the same as they had gone in. Nothing rots to a child. I didn't understand the point of the story was that they wouldn't.

In Michigan, the industry of Indiana faded into open fields and wood-lined roads. On rises I could see the lake curving to the opposite shore of our home.

We stopped at a turn-off and ate our sandwiches on the beach, wind driving sand into every bite. We swatted at the black flies chewing our ankles. After lunch, my father walked to the edge of the lake and stood there, as if waiting for something to happen. I watched him. I closed one eye, then the other, moving him in a shuffle from side to side. It was the only movement he made and I had made him do it.

Late in the morning we pulled into a farm. The sun had burnt off the sharp spring air. My skin warmed in small pricks. An old gambrel-roofed barn sagged in the middle. The clouds moved quickly in the sky, rising then falling and tumbling over one another in a ballet. They were the heavy clouds only a lake could birth.

We walked the split rail fence separating the dusty road from the yard of an old white house. The yard was patchy with grass and thistle but was mostly sand. An old woman walked from the house, shading her face from the sun, then turned back into the house and a few moments later reappeared wearing tall boots and a mesh cap.

"You the man with the new mare?" she said.

My father looked at me then at her. "Yes. We've come from Chicago this morning to see her."

The woman studied my father for a moment, then studied me. She pulled in her lip, biting hard.

"What type of cowboy you fancy yourself then?" she asked me and laughed. She was heavily bronzed and I wondered if between her deep wrinkles her skin would look like tiger fur.

She turned back to my father. "She's a live one but she'll break." She led us past the old barn toward a long and low sloped building. waves of heat rose above its tin roof.

We walked a long corridor of stalls, each the size of my bedroom and each with a horse eating or resting or shitting. It does not take long to know what a horse does and what a horse wants. Several heads protruded out the stall's Dutch doors and they looked like mounts on a wall, hunting trophies. Near the end of the corridor the lady slowed and took a lead and halter from a brass hook and peered into a stall. She slung the tack over her shoulder and snapped open the door bolt, making kissing noises as she slipped inside. My father lifted me to his shoulder. The woman stroked the mane of the horse and then slowly slid the halter over the horse's long muzzle and ears. She led the horse to the door and into the corridor.

"Sixteen hands. Good size Budyonny I'm told. Though I've never had this breed here. Never seen one 'til you got her shipped over. She's pretty ain't she?"

My father studied the horse. I asked if I could pet it and he leaned me in closer and I ran a hand down its long snout. Her chestnut hair was coarse and rough and oily. I scratched her nose above her flared nostrils and she pushed her head into my hand. My arm bent under her mass; she was strong. Her black eyes searched me. Her ears swivelled forward to catch the clang of tack rattling down the corridor.

"She's a bit new to this," the lady said and pulled back on the lead moving her head from near ours. "But hell, what do you say we give the little lady a ride, huh?"

The horse jerked her head up in a quick motion but the lady held firm and arrested the sudden jerk with a snap of the line and the horse huffed and raised and lowered a hind leg. The lady put a weathered hand on the horse's neck and ran its length in a slow rhythmic motion.

She led the horse outside to a rounded pen.

"Keep your distance back there. She'll split your knee in two in an instant if you try her."

The fence rails were made of thin trees nailed to vertical stumps buried in the ground. A few rails had split in the middle and lay in a V shape touching the ground. It did not look like a place that could hold a wild horse.

She pulled the horse in close and adjusted its halter and scratched under the thin band circling its ear.

The lady turned to me. "Come on, let's get you up."

I looked at my father but he did not look at me, I could find no confirmation, no explicit permission in his face. He was lost in the beauty of the horse. The world he had made in his head became real for him and in his face I could see the story became a myth. Here he was, a child of two dead Italian immigrants who had lived his entire life in a small neighbourhood of Chicago's west side, knowing only the world as it came in through the flat screen of the television and the pages of newspapers. It was the first and last time he could place himself in the story he told.

The lady's rough hand waved me toward the mare.

"Never cross behind her," she warned and pulled me close to her side as she told the horse to stay. She lifted me onto the horse's back. My legs splayed around its back and stretched my knees.

"Just rest your hands on her back," the lady said and she began to lead the horse in small circles that soon widened to the perimeter of the corral.

"Easy," the lady said. "Easy." To me or the horse or both I was not sure. The horse's dun hair was greasy and earthy and as my hands slide across its withers it picked up the scent of the animals. Its coarse black mane scratched my wrists. My insides shook with each quick step.

"What's the reason for you getting this horse?" the lady asked my father. "You a breeder or racer?"

I expected my father to start his story of the ice horses. I tightened as I waited for him to ask her if she knew why ice does not always freeze when it is supposed to. I felt my hands grip the horse's mane. I waited for him to explain how this was the same breed as the Russian war horse, that this horse was a descendent of the clan frozen in a lake on that arctic night but he did not tell her his story. He did not tell her any story. He stared through me as I trotted a circle over and over.

"I," he paused at a loss for an answer to this question. "I just needed to know it exists," he said.

We rode in silence back toward the city. I wanted another salami sandwich and another soda. I wanted to stop at the beach again. But we didn't. He sent the monthly boarding fees and talked on the phone to the lady, getting regular updates on the mare's health, her conformation, her training. The lady asked if he wanted to breed her but my father never said yes. He never saw the horse again.

It became a wedge between my parents.

"What the hell are we going to do with that horse?" my mother would ask, half rhetorically, half accusatory. "You going to butcher it like you do those hogs? Isn't that all you know how to do with a damn animal anyway?"

I would ask my father if we could see her again. I wanted another day at the beach, another soda and salami sandwich. I wanted that version of my father again. But he always had an excuse, a reason not to leave the city, not to leave the small enclave of our neighbourhood.

I moved on. To junior high school, to boys, to rebelling, to late-night underground punk shows where the world of dark and light collide and we do the things we have to do to make us *us*. I split space between my father and me, my mother and me. It became my life. I would climb down the metal fire escape in the back of the house after my father had gone to bed drunk. I would smoke weed outside the clubs. Show forged documents to the bouncers. I'd debate the stylistic merits of the Sex Pistols with men nearly twice my age. Sometimes I'd get drunk with them. At times I'd fuck them. Other times I'd just sit on the metal shelf outside my window in the winter and watch the light snow fall to the alley below. Sometimes I would open my mouth and catch a snowflake, thawing its brief moment in this world on my tongue.

One night not long ago I was watching TV and stopped at a nature special about horses. It had been years since I had thought much about them, years since I thought of my father's story, years before my brother and Lake Ladoga and the old lady and the green ribbons of the arctic sky tying themselves around the freed manes of the Russian horses running once again into another story.

There were long shots of wild mustangs running through the desert, some place out west like Nevada or Utah. Horses went extinct in the Americas about twelve thousand years ago the narrator stated, coinciding with the arrival of the first humans. "What drove them to extinction?" I wondered. Was it the changing climate, the ice sheets? Was it as simple as competition for food with the newly arrived humans? Or was it those early humans hunting the beasts into thin air because they could not yet see their utility, could not in their nascent wisdom find a bond, a compact with them, to build worlds and end empires. Cortez and his nineteen horses. Their march from the sea seeding a new old place with the potential of the domestic beast. Its face the end of times to those first people watching his armies crest a hill.

They would not reappear in the Americas until the Columbian exchange, the narrator stated, and even then, after they took to their native habitats once again, the indigenous peoples did not have a word for them and refused to give them one.

Then the phone rang and it was some distant thing that for years I too had not given a name.

The Mice

I left L.A. early the next morning and rose into a near clear sky. I had been living for years on a coast free of the Chicago cold. It was as far as I could get from home. Below I could see the earth unroll. The Sierras gave way to the high desert plains and I could make out the white salt flats below, whiter than mountain snow. The front range of the Rockies smoothed into plains, the earth moved from the angular ruggedness of wilderness to concentric circles and the plain weave of gingham fields shaded some colour of life in a cycle. The fields were golden and green, brown and bronze and they touched one another in crossroad nodes and by doing so became one giant chain stretched over the plains. Rivers oxbowed their way through the geometry of agriculture and the geological cacophonies only interrupted by the steel of small cars dotting their way along roads. And giant machines lumbered from south to north harvesting crops as if the whole weave of America might become undone, each wheel and turn of the thrasher pulling a single thread and unraveling the entire quilt only to have it sewn back up again in the spring.

Chicago was the Chicago I remembered. Damp and oily, the air wrung from the lake. It was late spring and in the shadows of buildings sank dirty brown snow slowly melting, water running along the sidewalks then freezing in the afternoon shadows. The city felt old and aged. It felt dated and forgotten.

I took a cab to Mount Sinai with the single small bag I had packed and found my father's room. A nurse scribbled in a chart, reading the wheeled monitor beeping in pulses. She stopped and looked at me, then searched the room and looked for someone behind me.

"Can I help you?" she asked.

"I'm," I began, "I'm his daughter."

She looked at my father as if his motionless body might give some suggestion that what I said was the truth but he did not move. She turned back to the chart and quickly finished what she had started.

"I'll leave you to him," she said.

I set my bag down on the floor and pulled up a chair wrapped in vinyl and sat next to him. I listened to the hiss of the oxygen filling his nose. Clear liquid swelled where the IV entered his wrist. His skin was loose, as if it had been accumulating and accreting like ice on a glacier all these years while the rest of him slipped away, melting where he meets the world. His eyes were closed and with each breath came a soft hiss. I could not bring myself to touch him, not yet, not after all these years. But I could tell his skin was the blue of an arctic lake. A game show whispered from the TV, a wheel spun, someone somewhere would be flying to Hawaii. I could not reconcile this dying man with the man I had rebelled against, the strong callous-handed butcher, a carver of flesh. It was as if the world were playing some cruel trick on him, so quickly what he had done to hogs was now being done to him. Time is as much a butcher as anything.

A doctor walked into the room. She was my age with red hair falling over her shoulder in a loose pony. She gave me a soft smile, not meant to comfort or reassure, then scanned his chart.

"You must be Curzio," she said.

"Yes, I'm Curzi."

"Sorry. Curzi." She closed the chart and slid it back into the pocket at the end of the bed. "Well, you were the only name listed here as next of kin contact."

"Isn't this something his home nurse should have taken care of?"

The doctor paused. Studied me. "Yes, well, his home nurse was the one who found him unresponsive the other day. He had a small stroke and I'm afraid there are no good options left."

"I don't understand." I said. "No good options?" I still had not understood why I was here. Why I had flown across the country for him.

"Curzi, you are here because there are no good options for your father. He did not leave a directive. You are here because we need someone to make a decision."

I turned and looked back at my father and studied his shallow breath. "Talk, God damn it," I wanted to say. "Talk, you stupid son of a bitch. Tell her your story. Tell her about the damn ice horses and how water can define the laws of nature. How about you do the same? How about you define the laws of nature and wake up, get yourself out of here." But I did not say this. I sat silently watching his face.

"Curzi, I know this is a lot. Someone will be in here shortly to check in on you. If you need anything let us know." And the doctor turned and left, and the hollow clicks of the pumps and machines filled the air.

I sat with him until dusk, through the quarter hourly checks. The nurses jotting notes, politely smiling, not saying what I knew they wanted to. I was waiting for their whisper, "turn it off." because turning the whole thing off is exactly what I wanted to do.

I took a cab to our old house on the westside. Nothing had changed. It was the same as the day I had left settled in time. The entryway's dark wood, the handrail on the stairs a richer patina now, worn over by my father's broken hands. It had been years since he had cut apart a hog, his fingers long ago bending into shapes which could no longer hold a knife. His muscles were undoing themselves, forgetting the patterns of his work he had spent years creating. He had come home one day and told our mother they had just quit and there was no use trying anymore and that was that. He sat around the house, watched TV moving from the news to old movies — classic westerns mostly. He watched them because of the horses, because of the hope he had of seeing his story turn true despite each one's desert setting. Lost in the boomeranged sound of the bullets he watched in glassy silence for a horse to enter some frozen creek in Montana, waiting for it to freeze the moment it enters.

The living room was the same except for a small twin bed in a corner. A table with pill bottles next to it; a medicinal kaleidoscope refracting the street lights outside. I picked a few up and studied the label; Malaparte, Antonio: Birthdate April 17, 1945.

I rummaged through the fridge for something to eat. Half empty cans of soups and olives. Milk a week expired. I found in the back a cheap can of beer hidden from his day nurse behind a box of baking soda.

I wandered the house and read his life — our life — as an archeologist might, looking for clues to piece the entire thing together. It was all shards to me like broken clay pots or fractured bones, some dirty cache of waste rearranged into a life, a museum. The fireplace, bricked up years before we lived in the house, still had the mantle of carved walnut and maple, its leaves and vines in tight knots climbing the side. A picture of my young mother, her eyes fixed just off camera, maybe to me or my brother perched on the stone hearth. I saw in her eyes a small fear. Maybe I was atop a slide or my brother on a swing, about to jump at the crest of the rise, both of us teetering on the edge.

Next to her a picture of the whole family, 1977. We were lean-ing against a yellow Buick with snow-capped mountains in the distance beyond. My brother's head resting on my mother's waist, his long arms hanging at his side. She has her arm wrapped around his shaggy hair, a palm over his ear. I'm standing in front of my father, his arms draped over my clavicle. He is the only one smiling. It's wide and bright, his thick black moustache trims his top lip, his eyes wide, near maniacal. It was a trip none of us wanted but him. We drove to Devil's Tower Wyoming then spent the next week in a draugthy cabin, no heat, no elec-tricity, fetching water and cooking over fire like pioneers. I'm not sure what we all were meant to get from it — connection to nature, connection to each other. I got a cold and spent three days in bed when we returned home. My brother got bitten by something in the night and scratched himself the entire drive home until he bled.

Between the pictures was the only artifact in the house dedicated to a horse. For how much my father had built his life around the story of the ice horses of Lake Ladoga, for how much time and money he had spent on having a horse of his own — the same breed as the Russian Calvary — boarded at a farm in Michigan, outside of his head there were no horses. There were no reminders of horses in the house except for the story he told and this single figure.

I picked it up and looked around the room, seeking its herd but it was all I could find. It was small, the size of my thumb, and made of porcelain. The bay-coloured paint was chipped and weathered. The front left leg had been broken off and it could not stand on its own. Its remaining three legs were locked in a gallop, the front leg bent like the letter C, its rear legs offset Zs. It looked like a relic of his childhood but I had never seen it. Maybe he had it hidden all these years in a drawer to keep it from me. Maybe he found it in a pile of thawing snow on a street corner, saved it before it fell into a puddle and froze during the night. Maybe it had been there all along, all these years and it was me who had not seen it, seen what was right in front of me the whole time.

I took the last warm swig of the beer. I had not eaten all day and the beer made me tired. I laid down on the couch and with the small horse in my hand, slept, fully clothed, with the lights on, until morning.

When I woke my lips were cracked. I was thirsty. For a moment, confused and lost in the house. I went to the sink for water and stood and drank over the basin. I drank again, thirsty from the flight and the hospital. I found some cheap coffee and a filter and started the drip machine and went back into the living room and searched my bag for new clothes. I found a sweater and underwear. I went for the shower. I passed the mantel and stopped. Between the picture of my mother and the picture of our family was the small porcelain horse, laying on its side as if it had never moved. Had I placed the horse there in the night? Did I not remember? I looked around the room for something else out of order — a television left on, glasses full of water — but I found nothing.

I showered and had coffee and sat staring at the house and all the things which made it. The photographs on the mantel. The porcelain horse. The twin mattress and the worn quilt and the orange bottles. The grey recliner with worn paths where my father had rubbed free the felt of the arm rest. There was a single thing I could do, just one thing and never again would I have to visit this place. Never again would I hear the story of the ice horses of Lake Ladoga echo in my head every time I passed a frozen lake. It was the reason I had moved to L.A. a place without snow, to escape things that froze. But there was no escaping it. In the house with the fading light of my father, there would never be an escape. There was only one thing I could do.

I finished the coffee and cleaned the pot and mug and repacked my bag. I hailed a cab to the airport.

On the flight to Stockholm, I read a copy of *National Geographic* I bought at a terminal store and drank a sparkling mineral water and ate a pack of sour gummy candies in assorted pastel colours. In the magazine, after an article discussing ducks and their sleeping habits (they sleep with half their brains at a time so as to stay aware of predators) I found an article on the melting permafrost of Siberia. Large swaths of the arctic tundra had begun melting, leaving in its wake pockmarked ground and craters. The largest was someplace in eastern Siberia in the taiga. It was nearly a kilometre long and over three hundred feet deep. It just opened one day, the earth giving way to itself. I thought about how much of that place must have been some in-betweenness, not really a frozen lake but not wholly earth either. An amalgamation of the two. I thought about the ocean and the shore, how one meets the other, how one slides over the other until it gets thinner and thinner and disappears into the other. But the taiga seemed some otherworldly place, a place where life didn't form, couldn't form. It was a place where millions of years ago some finned creature swam its way ashore, looked around, and went back. It was both this and not this at the same time. Ice, then earth, then ice, then earth, repeatedly layering on top one another in a frozen symphony of symbiosis. But it did not matter to me in that moment what might happen to the taiga in the future. I knew I wouldn't be around to witness it. What mattered was whether or not any of it would freeze once again for me.

I landed mid-afternoon in Arlanda and took a train to Stockholm. The train was clean, grey. An intercom announced something in Swedish. Flat and red houses blurred by. I closed my eyes against the window.

Stockholm rose from small granite bluffs. The train emptied into the low-slung buildings, onto the granite cobbled streets. The city floated on islands dotting the sea. Everything designed to disappear into the background.

I had an address, several years old, and not until I emerged did I panic. Was the address correct? I still had my single bag, the same clothes I had when I left L.A. three days ago. I was a half world away. Baroque church spires rose behind mansard roofed brick buildings. Nothing taller than three or four storeys. Blue and white ferries moved under the iron bridges; ice jammed in a few pockets along the shaded side of a blocky canal way.

I crossed a bridge to the old city, its iron railing once painted a blue or green. Across the bridge the road narrowed and rose to a church. I stopped at a window filled with antiques: crystal chandeliers, gold pocket watches and jewelled broaches. Opera glasses and china painted in the style of the Ming dynasty. Unwanted treasures from an age before this. I asked an elderly couple in English for the street. I found it somewhere deep in the centre of the city. The street was no wider than my outstretched arms. Graffiti lined the walls, purple and gold laced acronyms.

I passed a small door, a plaque in Swedish and English read "Brewer's Guild. Founded 1771." I found the address and took the stairs to the third floor. I was not sure what to expect, what it was I was going to do if he had not been there. If the address was wrong or old or vacant. I rang. He opened the door. There was something to tell him but I didn't speak. He watched me watching him. I wanted to speak but I said nothing. He waved me in.

"You know why I'm here Candido, don't you?" I used his full name, the name he hated as much as I hated mine. He flinched when I said it.

"Fuck, Curzi. You know I hate it."

When Candido was in high school he changed his name to C. He shed everything but a single letter, the first marker of what had once been there. He shed our father the same as his name, the same as me. But he slipped past us like a tide slips into the sea. While I crested like a wave, drowned out the family, drowned out the story of our father, C dissolved. He became less and less of himself and of us. And then one day, he was gone.

C took a jacket off a hook.

"Set your bag down.

We sat under a heater on a thin and curving road. Across the street were lines of small shops, a gallery with few paintings, a store selling kitchenware. On the corner was a grocer lost to time. Fowl hung by their necks in its windows like a Cotán painting.

"So, he's dead?"

"Nearly."

"Nearly? What does that mean?"

"What it means. I don't think so. Not yet."

C leaned back against the wall of the restaurant and took a long drink of his beer. He set the glass back on the table and spun it slowly, tracing the diamond-shaped relief of its body with his fingers.

"So you just got on a flight to Stockholm then?"

It was a rhetorical question. I didn't answer. We sat parallel to one another watching people pass. A mother in a hijab pushed a stroller, her small son stopping to pick up rocks every few feet. three teenage girls walked by, laughing at the shared screen of a phone.

"I had your address," I said. We sat silently for a while. Drinking, watching. What we said we said reflexively. What we meant we held internally.

"Do you know when he is going to die then?" C asked.

"He might have already, I'm not sure. Listen, I was named. I am the one who has to make the decision."

"Well, it can't be that hard." He washed down his bitterness with another drink. He started to clear his words. "All I'm saying is he was what he was. He did what he did. It doesn't mean what it has to mean, some bond tight as blood. People in this world have families, have children. It's how we make more people. Hell, it's just biology by another name. He made us and that's enough, I guess. We don't have to lionize the man."

"I'm starting to think I like the model where we make the people without the family part."

C snorted. "Still sharp."

"I know. I'm not keeping him alive for the sake of it. He had to have known, you or me, either of us would have done him in. I figured he'd have given it to the nurse or whoever. She might have had a bit more compassion than the two of us. But I've been thinking about that. Why did he make it me? I think he knew. I think he wanted, you know, in a time like this to just go. He didn't want any hesitation and so it landed on me. He knew I would do it except I didn't. I haven't, I mean. I can't."

The waiter walked to the table and C asked for two more beers. "Ett glas till," then pointing to both of us, "två." The waiter disappeared through the door and into the restaurant. We traced the path of a slow tug passing over the water between a row of buildings. A few moments later our beers came.

"Shit. Why not?" C said. "To dad." We raised our glasses.

"OK. Dad's dead. Or dying. Whatever. And you're here. A sister I never hear from, and then…what? You could have called. Saved a flight."

"I know. I'm not here just to tell you dad is dying."

"Really? Then why are you here?"

"You know the story of the ice horses…"

C cut me off. "Oh Jesus, come the fuck off it. Who on all of Taylor Street doesn't know that fucking story?"

"Right. But who really knows it? I mean, I know it. You know it. Dad knows it — knew it. It's all made up, right? Some fabrication for the ages. Not a single clear-headed scientist will tell you it's true. But not a single clear-headed person knows it is not *not* true either, right?

"I don't know where this is going but I don't like it. Not a bit."

"Dad's dying. Mom's dead. The house, whatever. The things will be sold, gone, displaced around the world, who knows. Who cares. But every time you see a horse, every time you see a frozen lake don't you in some small recess of your mind think for a split second, *maybe*?"

At this C lost it. "Believe it? Not for a second!" He laughed.

"You can't possibly tell me in all honesty you believe a bit of that garbage, can you? I mean, it's a story! No — it's a lie! He was a nothing person with a nothing life and that was all he had." C began to point his finger at the table, tapping with each word. "He told that story because that was the thing that made him a person in this world. That was the thing that made him material."

I nodded but said nothing. C let out a sigh and leaned back against the wall. We sat for a while watching an old couple shuffle to a table across the square and sit. I took in the radiant heat from above on my face. I felt flush. I felt the beer and blood rushing to my face.

"I'm going to do it." I said.

"Do what?"

"I'm going to do it. The whole thing. The fire, the horses. I'm going to do it."

I could see C spin in his head, looking for some way to snap lines into shapes. He put his forehead into his palm, he stuttered a few sounds.

"You're going to do? As in you're going to find a horse and put it in a lake and then what? Then what Curzio? Jesus Christ."

"Not a lake," I said, "*the* lake. Not *a* horse, all of them."

"Holy shit. You've lost your fucking mind. You've lost your goddamn mind." C stood and spun around. He stood reading my face then found something in the distance and fixed his stare to it. I waited for C to leave but he didn't.

"So let me get this straight. You fly halfway around the world to tell me that dad is either dead or dying but you don't know which and that you are going to go to Lake Ladoga, round up a thousand horse, then wait for the coldest cold of a thousand years and light a forest on fire and run them into the lake just so you can watch them drown, just for the satisfaction of *not* seeing the lake freeze solid in an instant? Just for the satisfaction of proving once and for all the falsehood of a dying man's story? Does that sound about right?"

I understood C's incredulity, his disbelief. Our father had abandoned us long before he died, long before our mother died. He had abandoned us slowly, each time he told the story of the ice horses, each time in his mind he saw that lake flash over in an instant. It became a world he wanted to live in, a world where there could be no absolute and no reason. A world built around a small seed of truth that once buried could grow into any number of things. I knew none of it to be true. I knew like the story, my father's life too was a lie. His name was not his name. His being not the being he wanted to be. But there was a small part of me that could not let the idea go. Maybe all possibilities are true and happening simultaneously, that no matter how remote the chance there is still a chance. I could not shake the thought of not trying. Whether or not that chance could ever exist in this world I didn't know but some part of me could not be put to rest until I knew.

"That's right," I said. "That is exactly what I am going to do."

"You're serious, aren't you?"

I nodded and finished the last of my beer. It had gotten dark and the heater was no longer keeping me warm. I said I wanted to leave. C didn't say anything more but paid for our beers and we walked through the narrow lamplit streets back to his flat. The closed store windows were illuminated by a single light, the outlines of their wares in the windows cast no shadows. The empty streets feel silent. The harbour lit at the edge of the city, a fog horn in the distance calling out.

"I don't know what to make of any of it anymore," C said.

He put his arm around me and hugged me tight at the shoulder. I started to cry. I could feel him do the same.

"You're crazy, you know that?" and he laughed. He wiped his eyes. "Fucking crazy." And then he muttered the last line of a dying man, "And in the spring the horses were free at last from their prison of ice."

That night I could not sleep. I was so tired from the jet lag and the travel I had somehow become untired, wide awake. In the early morning around two or three I got up from the couch and walked to the window. It was dark and a slight wind moved the backlit flags on the harbour. I stood for a while overlooking the water. The sky was clouded over and the yellow lights of the city lit their underbelly. My legs were tight. I was restless.

I dressed and wandered the streets alone. I walked without intention. Everything was new and old at the same time. I held no reservation and I thought about a dying man thousands of miles away. Somehow Stockholm felt familiar. There was something about the streets, the cobbled lanes and the granite buildings, the tiled roofs that felt distant yet close, that felt hidden yet seen. I walked past the Royal Palace and under a white light a lone guard stood watch, his gaze fixed on some distant point only he knew. I walked close to him and smiled but he did not notice or was well trained enough not to.

I crossed a bridge crowned with golden crests and the full briskness of the cold hit me. I tucked my hands under my armpits and lowered my neck fully into my brother's jacket. The iron rail was specked with locks locked on locks. I thought of the lovers, how many of them were still out there. How many were still in love?

I found a lonely stretch of road sheltered from the wind and walked past museum after museum. I had read about several of them in the in-flight magazine: The Abba Museum, the Vasa Museum with its old ship slowly rotting. I passed Tivoli, the walled amusement park, and though it was closed I could hear the screams of riders on the roller coaster and the tin jingles of the games. We had never once as children visited such a place but I knew what they looked like and I pictured Tivoli all the same. There would be rings to toss, bottles to knock over. Large stuffed animals. Cheap trinkets lost or broken before the day was through.

The wind whipped a yellow cross in a field of blue and I counted the yellow filamented bulbs that made the word "Tivoli" above the arched entrance. Then I heard the horses. The unmistakable sound of metal shoes hitting stone. The sound was arrhythmic; it was several horses out of sync, stepping at their own pace. I looked around but no one was on the street. A few cars crossed the bridge and passed near. I heard the horses again. I walked to the far end of the white wall and turned a corner and saw three white horses being led by a small girl in a yellow dress. She was leading them toward the harbour, toward a line of green and red fishing boats and I watched as they passed through the street and disappeared beyond the far wall of the amusement park. I looked around for some witness but there was none. A taxi slowed and the driver bent toward the passenger door and waved at me. I shook my head. The taxi sped off.

"They're pretty, aren't they?"

I spun around. Across the street a man was leaning against the wall of a restaurant. I could make out the outline of its menu over his shoulder.

"What?" I asked.

"I said they're pretty. They're the royal horses, you know. The Kings."

"You saw them?"

"Sure I saw them. They're here most nights."

I turned back to look for the horses or some trace of them again but I didn't see anything.

"They're gone now. You could probably see them tomorrow again if you want. Almost always the same time too." He pulled something from his pocket and put it in his mouth, a small dime-sized packet. "You lost or something? A tourist right?"

"Something like that."

"Thirsty? You haven't seen Sweden yet until you've had some schnapps. Come on. I'll buy you one."

I looked around but the street was still deserted. I thought about running. I could make it over the bridge and back to my brother's apartment in minutes. Who was this man?

"Eugene. I got a name. See." He pulled out an ID and walked toward me. I froze. "See?"

I looked at the ID. It was a driver's license from California.

"Me, you. Expats. I got a place we can go around the corner. I'm sick of trying to speak Swedish. Come on. Let's get some schnapps."

A narrow stone stairway tucked in an ally led to an underground room. Inside, it was dark and a few people sat at a table in the back corner. A bartender stood scrolling his phone behind what looked like a temporary bar. Eugene ordered and brought the drinks over to the table.

He had the beers and the two shots squared in his hands. "Here," he said and set the shots down carefully then split the two beers between us. "It's real shit. Tastes like ass. But the Swedes love it."

I smelled the liquor and it smelled like black liquorice.

"Rough," I said.

"Skol." And he tipped it back.

I sniffed mine and took a small taste. "Oh, that is bad." And pushed it aside.

"What's your deal," he asked. "You new here?"

"No, I'm just visiting my brother. I couldn't sleep."

"Me either. This town is so goddamn boring you think it would constantly be knocking you out like some drug but it doesn't. I found this place late one night when I couldn't sleep. Just kind of stumbled into it."

"I didn't know bars were open so late here."

"They're not," he said and started on his beer. My small sip of schnapps had made me warm. The wind from the harbour had left me chilled. I felt my cheeks begin to glow. Eugene looked around the place as if he might know someone but I could tell he didn't. He caught the eye of one of the people sitting at the far table and gave a small nod and she nodded back but then turned back to their conversation. His head stuck out from his body in a stork-like manner, long and awkward in the space it occupied. He was less threatening than threatened, some prey bird scanning the sky for predators, constantly surveilling the world above him. I felt a little sorry for him. He seemed as lonely as I was. As lost in the world as any person might find themselves in a foreign place.

"Do you like it here?" I asked.

"Meh. It's good and bad. It's also a job."

I didn't enquire about his job. I didn't care. I wasn't interested in what IT department he worked in or what coding language he used. Stockholm was awash in the world outside the world we lived in, the interconnected coded places we turn to more and more.

"So just visiting your brother? How long are you here then?"

Eugene had not thought he might get this far, he had not thought I would have followed him to this place and now I could see he was lost, swimming in his head for places to dive.

"Just a few days. I won't be around long."

"Yeah, heading back to the States?"

His eyes were narrow and distant and when he looked at me he seemed to look right through me. He had a small crack in his lip and he pulled a tube from his pocket and spread it over the cracked spot.

I felt relief, I felt I could say whatever I wanted to him because I would never see him again. I would never have to remember his name or his face or the way he chewed on the inside of his cheek after every sip of beer. He would just glimmer past me like everyone else.

"Do you really want to know?"

He took a sip of beer then set the glass down. "Sure. OK."

"Russia. I'm going to Russia."

"Russia? Yeah, OK. What's in Russia?"

And here, in this underground and most likely illegal speakeasy in the centre of Stockholm, I told the story of the ice horses of Lake Ladoga for the first time. I told it just the way my father had. I remembered every detail. The questions, the dates, the look of terror as the horses froze in a carnal mass, instantly, in the blink of an eye. I told him about the firebombing of the forest, how when ice freezes that quick it screams as if it too felt the pain of instant death. I told it like I believed it. I told it like it was my story.

When I finished, I looked around the bar and Eugene looked down at his near empty glass.

"That's wild. I didn't know ice could do that."

"It can't."

"What?"

"It can't. It doesn't. The whole fucking thing is made up."

Eugene looked at me. He didn't understand the point of the story. He didn't understand why I had told it and to be fair, neither did I. I had told him I was going to Russia. I had told him the reason. I had led him through the story of the ice horses and then I had told him I didn't believe a word of it.

I will say this about Eugene. None of it fazed him. The horse, the ice, my lies or my plans. He bought us another round of beer and we sipped them silently for a long time. He nodded to a distant beat, some Swedish techno from a speaker at the far end of the room. I lost track of the world outside the hot cellar.

"You know what I know?" he finally asked. "About the war? This place was the only civilized place left. I mean Sweden. You could leave your lights on here. Someone told me that once. They didn't pick a side. I mean they did by not fighting, but life just kept on going as normal as it could. I've never thought much about it. It doesn't mean anything to me. Your story might have been the first time I actually thought about what it was like then. It's wild shit."

Eugene was getting drunk and I was too. My time in Sweden had so far been framed by one beer to another and I was feeling sick. I didn't want to be in there anymore. I needed fresh air.

"Have you ever seen the movie *The Bicycle Thief*?"

I closed my eyes and the room spun. "I don't feel good," I said, "I need some air."

"Yeah. Sure," Eugene said and finished the last pull of his drink and we walked to the street. The cold breeze off the harbour levelled my head. I stood facing the water looking at its blackness, listening to it blindly lap the canal walls.

"The movie, it's about this guy who has his bicycle stolen then he has to steal another bicycle. It's a movie about cycles. About how everything is all chained together. It's supposed to be one of the best movies ever. It's in black and white but it's still pretty good."

I wanted to leave. I needed to sleep. I was jet-lagged. I told Eugene I had to go. He was swaying, his eyes resting in long blinks. I started for my brother's apartment.

"Wait," Eugene said. "I was going to tell you about the movie."

"What?"

"I was going to say that it's like your horse story. You said it was your dad's story and now you're telling it. It's like the movie, see? It's all we do, right? Lose something that's ours then take something to fill its place." He cycled his arms like he was pedalling a bike, stumbled, then gripped the rail for balance.

I turned toward the canal. "Nice to meet you, Eugene. Thanks for the drinks." And I left him swaying there near the harbour.

I woke in the morning past nine. The heavy clouds hanging over the harbour had burst open in the night and a light rain was still falling on the city. C was making coffee and toast. My head pounded. It hurt to open my eyes.

"Did I miss anything?" I asked.

"Miss anything? There is nothing to miss in this city. About the only thing you missed is the few hours of daylight we get." He pulled the toast from the toaster and buttered each slice then spread a red jam over the butter. His apartment was sparse. A few chairs, a TV, the couch I slept on. A single poster hung on the wall in the style of those old French travel ads from the 1930s, a blocky man and a woman looked over their shoulder toward a bullet train crossing a canal.

"It's a bit cliché don't you think?"

He looked out from under the upper cabinets. "Huh?"

"I mean this place. It looks like a damn IKEA catalogue."

"Oh," he said. "Welcome to Sweden."

He brought me over a coffee and toast.

"Jesus, what did I drink last night?"

"It's the jet lag," he said. "You're probably still dehydrated. I'll get you some water." He turned and headed back into the kitchen then returned with a glass and sat on the chair near the end of the couch.

"I had the weirdest night," I said.

C took a bite of his toast and crumbs fell into his lap. He stuck his neck out and looked down, pulled his shirt tight and swept them onto his plate.

"Yeah? Some wild dreams?"

"Not dreams. I took a walk last night, over the bridge to the island with the museums."

"Djurgarden? No, you didn't."

"Yeah, I was walking near Tivoli and I saw this little girl in a yellow dress leading three white horses toward the harbour."

"You dreamed it. You were out cold last night."

"No. I left and walked around the city. It was freezing, I remember."

"Impossible," C said. "The door locks automatically at night. The one downstairs. The entry door. You need a key to get in." C took a drink of coffee and then another bite of his toast and walked to the back bedroom. "Unless you stole these last night from my room," and he set the keys on the table.

"Maybe the door was unlocked?"

"Maybe, but I doubt it. Swedes keep a pretty tight ship." He laughed a little at his own joke. I felt off balance. I *had* walked the night before. I had walked to Tivoli, seen the lights, talked to the taxi driver. Three white horses and the girl in the yellow dress. Eugene. I had told the story I never wanted to tell. It had all happened.

C finished his toast and leaned back in his chair and brought his coffee cup toward his face and let it rest under his nose, the steam filtering up and over his eyes. I couldn't tell if he was lying. If he was leading me on, but I was too tired. I let it pass. Took a bite of my toast. Drank my coffee. We sat in silence watching the city wake through his windows. The spire of the city hall rose through the clouds, the black and orange roofs of the building between us, damp and dripping. C refilled my coffee.

"You were serious, weren't you? Last night. You're actually going to do it?"

I had thought about it in the way you think of something abstractly, as if it will only ever be an outline or a frame, lines of relief but never a shadow. In my mind, the plan was a perfect copy of the imagined world. But once I spoke it out loud telling C about it the night before it was if it had become illuminated, every contour now lit.

"I am," is all I said, all I could say. Speaking it had made it something real.

"Do you have a ticket? How are you going to get into Russia? Do you have a visa?"

"Fuck C." I rubbed my forehead, digging the tips of my fingers into the dull throb. "I'll figure it out."

"Do you have a job? I mean, still? What about dad? Did you make the call?"

"Jesus, when did you become the fucking cops. I'll pack my bags and go. I'm not looking for an interrogation." I stood suddenly and a sharp pain filled my ears and pressed my eyes shut tight.

"Yeah, OK. OK. Relax. I'm sorry. I didn't mean to start in so early." C poured himself another cup of coffee.

"I'm in," he said. "I'm kind of burnt out on this place anyway."

"What?"

"I said, I'm in. I was in last night, at the bar when you said it. I just needed to know if you were serious."

"Wait, you mean…"

"You know I heard the story as much as you did. Maybe more. I thought it was a total crock of shit too. But dad. You couldn't get him to move. It was impossible." C paused. He was impossible. He never thought it was untrue. Some people, they know — or maybe they think they know — it's a crock of shit, whatever story they tell themselves to get through the day. They stand their ground but just to stand on something. Fight for something however stupid it makes them sound. But dad, he just didn't have that. You would challenge him and he would stare at you, like you were the lost soul, you were the one wandering the desert." C paused. "A pious prick, you know? Like he was the one carrying the cross. Like he knew the suffering first-hand. Looking back, it's hard not to pity him."

A muffled horn passed off the water. Soft voices rose from the alley below. "So you're in? As in *in*?" I asked.

"That's what I'm telling you."

I looked at C and I saw him for the first time as a shadow of our dad. He was washed in grey. His hair, his thin nose, his eyes. He was without colour, he had become tints and shades. Black and white. It was as if I were staring at an image of what I thought my brother would never look like. And then I worried about the fire, about the windswept inferno I was willing to ignite in the Lake Ladoga wilderness and I worried about my brother, adding what little light he might to that fire, burning like a candle.

The Dogs

It was late spring and the sun was now burning off the slow days of winter. We had packed heavy. Tents and guy lines, rainflies and stakes. We bought boots sealed against rain and winter. Crispbread and pickled fish. Dried fruit. Maps. I bought rope for makeshift halters and leads.

We caught a bus through Upplands, through the flat clay-rich lowlands shouldered with smooth granite boulders and hills. It was an old sea floor, once a place where creatures swam. From the jutty tip of the Swedish east coast we took a ferry through the waters that separate the Baltic from the Bothnian Seas to Åland.

I found a copy of *Kaputt* by Malaparte in a used bookstore before we left Stockholm. The owner of the store studied the book as if it was not from his collection. If he made any connection between the book and the name on my credit card he did not show it.

I had never read the book because it was the book that most drew my father back to the old continent. He had for his whole life been living in some liminal space, always crossing a threshold. Conceived in the old world, born in the new. He carried a photo with him of his parents leaning against the side of an old round-hooded car with solid hubcaps. His father is grinning wide-mouthed at his mother, her eyes fixed to the shutter. It was only days after they had come to America. It wasn't even their car. It had been borrowed. These were his parents, the ones whose name he gave away and took another, separating again his life into a blurred line run as some boundary on a map. He took the name Malaparte as if to remain something here and something there.

For Malaparte the author there could be no separation between the aristocracy and the suffering masses, there was no here or there in war. Over roast roe deer and fowl, drinking wine the masses did not know existed, his war disappeared. It disappeared like my father's father's war did when he moved to America. It disappeared in the distance between what once was and what had become, a new life, a purpose. My father took this — he became someone new but he also remained straddling an ocean. As I read the book I could not help but read my father onto Malaparte, fascists until the end, hiding their way into America through false allegiances to a flag that was soon to fly over half of Europe. He — they — were fascists before they knew what it could mean, before I could understand the terror and totality of it. In the moments when I truly hated my father, I would let fly the words I knew he hated to hear. I called him that name. He wasn't ashamed to be one but he was ashamed to have it spoken into the world. As if holding onto the words would allow him some soft escape if he needed it. I knew this feeling. I think we all do. We hold on tight to a few words, let them echo in our heads only.

We never speak them. We use them as our entry points into a different world. We tell ourselves a story with them, rearranging their sounds to make some new meaning, untranslatable even to ourselves.

I woke up somewhere in Finland, the gentle rocking of the sea still buried in my ear. The ferry had buffets and booze, but I ate little and drank less. The clanging of nickel slot machines drowned out the low drone of the diesel engines.

I was sick. Part with fever and part with sea. I asked C where we were. "Somewhere near Helsinki," he said. "We'll get some rooms there."

Helsinki, for what it was, was a fever dream. I moved in some otherworldly state and found nothing and took nothing. We slept in a hotel near the bay. I could hardly move. I laid and stared at the deep cracks in the ceiling. I traced the valleys in the plaster over and over. The old windows, small panes and lousily glazed in their wells, let in the cold breeze off the bay. I passed through visions of forest and horses. My fever disappeared the water, the ice. A trough of nothing filled the space where the lake had been. I called out for him, but I got no answer. C told me we should find a doctor but I was too ill to argue or agree, and with no decision, I spent the night sliding between what might have been and what might soon be near.

I sweated through the night in a purblind sea, and then, so heavy with fever I fell away and did not return for three days. I was in a place I did not know and could not recall. I thought of our father, alone in the hospital room. I heard the clicking in my ear of a mechanical machine, something designed without the dying in mind. I was everywhere and everything.

I thought of our mother. I thought of her long suffering and her swollen eyes. I could taste in my chalky mouth the sweet sauces she made. The fragile cookies we ate at Christmas and Easter. She was no less Italian than my father, born and raised in that same small square of Italy outside Italy in Chicago. In the night I was with her again, in the summers of my youth, with her and her sisters at our grandparents. C and I would listen to the fast Italian being shouted across the room. Our cheeks would be patted and pinched and our stomachs tested for ripeness. It terrified us completely. And then we would return and we watched as my mother turned from that rich golden hour above the sea to the washed winter clouds hugging the coast. She would move slower and slower and become a decoration, a trinket in every room she passed through and then, one day, she wasn't even that. She had been broken while someone dusted the corners of the curio cabinet, broken into a million tiny pieces. In my dream, I tried to piece her back together, the shards cutting my fingers.

Death cannot separate what is, what was, and what will be. In those days before I knew what death was but felt it near, it did not panic me. I knew the last thing we lose before we leave this place is our hearing, we let go of the world outside us and turn in. We can close our eyes, we can deny ourselves food, but we cannot stop the world from vibrating. I knew as I lay there, in the bricked walls of a rundown Helsinki hotel, that in those moments before death the smallest bones in our body will refuse to move and in this refusal they will fuse into one, larger bone. A statue to the world we once could hear. We will be left with a ringing that fades into the ocean, the purl of a boundary from which we came; not sea, not land, but a place where states unknown mix, where states unknown find a divinity unreachable, unlike anything humans have carved into stone. In those last moments of our life, a life made of the stories it had told itself, we cannot hear a story being told.

Before the fever breaks, in my mind I walk to the Helsinki shore and I find my father and I watch him slip into the sea. He is naked, and his bloated body, swollen from years of neglect, becomes some leviathan figure. He slips past me and into the primordial place. A place without words, without the separations that make words. It is a place of the ambient. The origin of myth. I watch him return.

C walks into the room with a few bags, some food, some supplies. He set them on the wooden table and began to unpack.

"C," I said. "he's gone."

"You're awake. I was getting worried."

"He's gone."

"Who? Dad? Did they call?"

I shook my head and C said nothing because nothing was needed. He continued to unpack and handed me a carton of food. He pulled out a topo map and unfolded it on the table. I sat up and studied it.

"I found us a way through, to the lake, here."

C pointed to a long, winding road and we traced its route together.

"Let's leave then. Tonight."

"Are you sure?" he asked.

"I can make it."

C weighed my face. I could tell he pitied me and I resented him for it.

"No, not that. Are you sure about dad?"

"No." I said. "But that's what makes ghosts so scary."

It was Midsummer in the far north and the sun would not set and would not for weeks. It lagged through the sky and briefly touched the horizon shortly before midnight. The nights were soft blue. We packed to leave our hotel. We drove toward the border, toward the wilderness, left to make sense of a world in light.

"This is it. I think." C pulled the car over and checked his phone. "There," and he pointed to a small lake just past a narrow bridge. "That's Russia."

"There? It's so close?"

"I'll pull over and park somewhere. I'll find a turnout." C started the Volvo and merged back onto the rust-coloured road.

"We're just going to leave the car? It's a rental."

"You worried about the late fee?" C says. "I don't think a late fee is our worry now. How long are we going to be? We'll be back in a few days."

C found a turnout and pulled the car in along some trees, off the road as if abandoned or forgotten.

"Might give us a few days before anyone starts to think something," he said.

"You used a pseudonym I hope."

"Oh yes. One of my many. I keep three different IDs for just such an occasion."

We took our packs and started toward the lake.

"The map shows maybe five miles, maybe a bit more. But I don't know what it looks like in there."

In my mind this place had been wilderness, an empty set of words. In my mind it had been a place still wild, and a place without names or objects or meaning. It had been a place seen but not counted, parcelled, broken into plots. The wildness of it couldn't be sorted.

By three we had neared the lake.

"I think it's right over the next rise or two," C said and we caught our breath. It was mid-July and the air was warm but the ground held close the chill of spring. Sea green and rust orange lichen covered the rocks, moss coated the north side of the bony spruce. We climbed a few rises and red granite boulders and then, through a clearing, saw a fjord leading to Lake Ladoga. We stopped.

Below us was the lake and it stretched as far as we could see and it did not want to end. The surface moved in small ripples and lapped at the blocky shores of the inlet. C set down his bag. I did the same.

"Fuck. Fuck," C said. He put his hands to his face and with them, washed something from it. He lathered some imaginary thing from his skin. "Why?"

I looked at him. "C," I said, but stopped.

"This is what you want to do? This is how you think it's going to end?"

"What are you talking about?"

"This," and he waved his hand over the lake like he expected some big reveal, some object in relief to appear before us. "This. All of it."

I knew what he meant. I saw it too. The lake was endless. On the map it looked contained, small next to the land around it. But here, on a ledge above the jelly green water it went on forever.

"This will never freeze." And he turned his back to me and stared over the water.

"Fuck you," I said. "I didn't make you come. You chose this. And don't blame me like your father would. You knew what this was."

"*My* father? Come off it, Curzi."

"No, where were you? Where have you been? I'm the one who had to deal with dad. I'm the one who had to go back there and rid that place of him."

"And look at you now. Thousands of miles away from him as he dies alone in a hospital room. You're no saint Curzio," C said.

Suddenly, as if the lake had already taken hold of me, I slipped past myself into some other place. My ears swelled with blood and started ringing. My stomach turned, the bitter rush of body pushed through me, I was nowhere and everywhere at once, and I watched myself walking toward him, and pushing him over the edge.

C swung his arms like windmills, like a cartoon brought to life, reaching for nothing, reaching for me, as he slid off the face of the rock toward the lake. I watched knowing in the moment all things in this world are final; time moves in one direction. Two magpies circled above and called to one another. They landed in a spruce along the shore. The tops swayed lightly. I fixed my eyes further up, away from the water to the far horizon, because instinct pushes you to turn away from an explosion.

C was laid out below. Everything about it was cartoonish. The fall. The scream. His ragged body. His twisted leg. The birds in endless circles above. I scrambled down the rock face. His pants were bloody. I saw the blunt end of a bone pressed against the nylon.

In the tenth grade, I trained in first aid and CPR; it was required to become a summer lifeguard at the community pool. We practiced on a rubber dummy named Annie. Through the thin plastic mouth protector I could smell the rubber skin, taste the bitterness of it. Between resuscitations we rubbed it down with alcohol. I remembered the coolness in my fingers as the alcohol evaporated from the white cotton swab. The boys joked about getting to third base, who could take it the furthest. They told us girls we were lesbians. They told us it was hot.

We took turns splinting each other's arms. We all would fake our screams of pain. "Sit still," we would tell one another. "But I'm dying!" we would laugh. We never splinted legs. That summer, we never saw anyone die.

"Is your friend hurt?"

I turned back and saw an old woman standing where we were a few minutes earlier, a dog by her side panting and staring down at us, its head cocked slightly to its side, one ear flopped over its head like an Aussie slouch hat. Between pants it whimpered. The woman told the dog to sit and it laid on its stomach, its head still leaned over the edge of the rock watching us.

"I think he's hurt pretty bad. He slipped and fell and I can't get him up." It was true, he did slip and fall.

"You will wait." And the woman and her dog disappeared. C's laboured breath pulsed slowly. I had the thought that if that woman had not shown I might have rolled C over the edge of this rock, into the water below. I doubted he could be saved, or I didn't want to believe I could save him. We were alone in the world. No one knew where we were. I felt sick at the thought. I could hear our father's words: "Anonymity dissolves all morality." My stomach turned. I puked a watery green bile.

I took my brother's hand and squeezed it. It was clammy; I leaned my head in to check his breath. I do not know if I was seeking it or seeking its end.

The woman came down the rock face first, followed by her dog. The dog ran over and sniffed me, then C, smelling closely the fractured point of the leg then pranced over to my puke and took a small lick and backed away. The dog squatted and urinated in the same spot.

"Heel," the woman commanded and the dog did nothing but ran back from where they came and traced some imaginary line along the ground.

The woman had a rustic travois fashioned from a few straight birch branches and some vine as webbing laced through the centre. She set it parallel to C on the ground.

"You'll have to take the legs," she said. I grabbed his legs and C winced in pain.

"Jesus, at the thigh," the old woman yelled and I adjusted my grip.

We lifted C onto the travois and the woman began to pull him up the path she had come down. The dog circled us, its black and white long hair was matted against its belly, caked with mud. It nipped at our heels as we pulled.

"Heel, no," the woman commanded but the dog did not listen and continued to herd us.

In a short distance, we came to the woman's korsu. I nearly walked over it without knowing. I was out of breath and sweated heavily. We set down C and I knelt and took off my pack and then sat on it. The woman disappeared into the korsu and then emerged with a bucket of water and handed it to me. I took a long drink. It tasted like iron and was heavy. The woman lifted the front of the travois and pulled C into the korsu and I watched as they disappeared into the dark. I took several drinks from the bucket and the woman returned and took the bucket from me, drank from it, then set it on the ground for the dog. I wiped my lips as the dog drank.

The korsu was hidden as if part of the forest, the only obvious entrance was the old wooden door. The stacked timbers had mostly been covered with a clay dapple and moss and lichen grew in patches on the side with the door. The rest of the structure disappeared into the hillside.

"I've called a doctor. Come in," she said and we entered the korsu.

Inside it was modern, walls finished to look like any house, smooth, painted. A sink with plumbing, a bathroom. The toilet was outside but a fully functioning shower stood in the corner. In the kitchen were wood countertops and a single outlet with a black charger connected to an old cell phone. The old woman poured a cup of tea and handed it to me. I cupped the chipped glass and took a sip. It was hot and tannic and tasted of birch and dirt.

The woman studied me and I favoured the tea, staring into the silty water. "He must have slipped," she said and did not look away from me.

"Yes. He was trying to take a picture and," I took a sip of tea. "And just slipped."

The woman nodded her head in agreement.

"This doctor," I said, "he is from around here?" It was a stupid question. I wanted to change the topic.

The old woman said yes, either ignoring the question or its

absurd basis. "Hospitals in Russia are not very good. If you want care you get it at home. He is very good."

"Your English is very good," I said.

"Of course. Everyone speaks English. And if they don't, they wish they did."

"You did not come to this place to fall either, did you?" and her question was pointed. I coughed on my tea. She stood and entered the kitchen and brought out the tea kettle and filled my glass again. I did not want more tea. I had not ceased sweating since the climb with the travois and the tea was making it worse.

"It is good for you to sweat," she said and placed the kettle back on the wood stove. The dog was scratching at the door and the woman opened it and the dog came in, panting, and ran over to sniff at my tea then my pants. The dog sat, then flopped to its back and pawed at the air and I scratched its belly.

"My name is Elli, Curzio. And this is my house. You are welcome to stay because I know you have no place left and because your brother is in the next room. I do not think he will survive, not out here. This is a wilderness. It does not care about you or me or your brother. But I will do what I can for him."

Her abruptness caught me off guard and I began to reel. Had I told her my name in the panic of moving C? Her korsu was close to the rock where C had fallen. She must have heard us arguing. She must have known he did not slip. I had a sudden urge to sprint from that place but I couldn't move. My skin flushed and my body froze.

"Elli? Thank you," I said and she looked past me toward the door. A few seconds later we heard a knock and the dog bolted to its feet and let out a sharp, single bark.

"The doctor," Elli said.

I slept that night in a nest of down and straw. My sleeping bag, new, red, filled with a layer of down was atop a web of rope and a tick mattress. I could not stop thinking of how I had gotten where I was. What had led me here. Before we left, I had taken a train to Uppsala while my brother readied himself for our trip. I walked the hill to Domkyrka, the twin spired church perched above the river. I had been restless, second guessing myself and the decision I had made to see it through. We had grown up catholic, a requirement of my father. My father the fascist sympathizer. The man who thought so highly of a government bent on scorning the pious. Our church in Chicago had been ordinary, nothing like the majestic cathedrals of Europe. It had been built sometime in the '60s, its low roof timber-framed with long, modern wood beams. The green carpet was worn thin in the aisles, the pew ends curled figures chipped and snapped along the grain lines. In the basement the white painted cinder blocks were lined with folding tables and plastic chairs. My brother and I would take pocketfuls of cookies after every mass, overly sweet store-bought sugar cookies with a token sprinkling of purple or red flakes.

When I entered the Domkyrka it was the first time I had entered a cathedral in Europe. It was nothing like our church back home. A few people walked among the alcoves and my footfalls echoed off the high stone walls. Every sound was magnified just as it was designed to do. I walked over catacombs and the stone carved names of famous Swedes. I heard voices sing from somewhere hidden: *Pie Jesu Domine / Dona eis requiem* and there was no doubt in my mind, in that moment, the world was tinder with nothing to do but burn.

The Birds

In the morning I woke crying my brother's name. The dog was curled at my feet, breathing deeply, whimpering in its own dream. I heard no movement. I rose and dressed and in the other room the old woman stood sipping the same tea she had offered me the day before. She presented it to me but I wanted coffee, anything but the tea. I thanked her and sat to sip the tea. I ate a piece of dark bread with her. We did not speak while the dog slowly ate a tough piece of flesh the woman had thrown on the floor. I did not ask to see my brother and she did not offer. There had been talk of money exchanged for the doctor's visit. I had gone to bed before he left, part because of exhaustion, part to avoid the reality of the situation. I was terrified of what I had done but more terrified that I had felt so little remorse. We all die, I thought. We all die. So what if it is by the choice of another? What does it matter how our earthly time ends?

"We will leave soon," Elli said and left the room and the dog trotted after her. I finished my tea. It was cool and without its heat it turned more bitter. I threw my last bite of toast onto the floor for the dog.

I stepped outside and a fog was lifting off the lake. A thin layer of wispy clouds hung in the sky. I tried to put a name to them, digging from the words from grade school, but I found none.

We left about noon. In the distance a church bell rang. I counted its twelve tones. Elli and the dog came outside and without a word of direction, started walking. The dog followed close, veering around the trees, tracking creatures that have long since disappeared. Elli moved slowly and stopped every so often to examine small mushrooms. Some were orange and spread like a fan and these she picked and placed in a shoulder bag sewn from an old T-shirt.

"You won't be leaving this place will you?" Elli asked but did not look at me. "It's like old age itself, you enter it but you will never leave it the way you entered." She kept her focus on the ground, looking for small forests of fungus. The dog barked quickly at something in a tree, then moved on. I was silent because I did not have an answer but I knew it was true. As C and I planned we discussed ferries and trains and cars and roads, all leading to the lake in the woods but neither of us had talked of a return. Neither of us had planned just how long we were to stay in this place. We understood that if we were to go through with the plan, burn the wilderness completely and freeze the lake, there would be no escape. There would be no end we could script and we both understood this.

Elli and I and the dog continued on and she stopped and picked mushrooms and placed them close to her nose and took in their deep smells. We walked the shore and my eyes were fixed on its low terrain, the shallow bays and sharp cliffs. I studied the trees, birch and pine and spruce, that grew on the watery edge.

I could feel Elli study me. I could feel her gaze when my back was turned.

"Do you know the story of Madonna of Wieliczka?" she asked.

I turned to face her, the dog was sniffing a spot she was searching on the forest floor and she pushed the dog away from the spot.

"I don't," I said.

"I will tell you the story then. In Wieliczka, deep underground there was a salt mine. Humans had been harvesting salt and surface brine since before they knew time. Before Christ, during Christ, after Christ. Miners mined salt, for how does a human body live without salt? But it was not enough to simply mine salt. Miners felt it was their holy obligation to also pay respect to their Lord and Saviour. For it was God and his only son that kept them safe and saw their safe passage through that dark and dangerous place.

"And so miners, they carved Madonna from salt. Miners would line up and pass by the salt statue everyday entering mine and then again when they left. The miners would remove their hats, and remove their candles, snuff out flame as they passed the Madonna statue.

Now, since the statue was made of salt, miners passed without crying. They could not cry because tears they shed might melt the statue. But this world," Ellie paused, picked another small orange fan from the earth and studied it. "This world is not a gentle place.

"Madonna has many reasons to weep. She weeps for her son. She weeps for the entire world. It is Madonna's holy obligation to care for burdens of suffering masses of desolate places. In one of these times of desolation, miners entered mine and saw Madonna was weeping. At night, they said she had begun to weep. Miners hurried and collected her tears; they drank them and they were, in fact, tears. They tasted of salt and they tasted of the world's sadness. Miners could not stop Madonna from weeping. Her tears came, no matter how much they prayed, how much they pleaded with the virgin mother to stop. They prayed for world peace. They prayed for universal love and compassion but Madonna only wept. They could not stop sadness. They took to the streets of Wieliczka and preached the Lord's gospel. They abandoned their lust, their sloth. They abandoned drinking and vodka. They found new meaning in their families.

But they could not catch all of her tears and soon her tears began to dissolve the salt from which she was carved. Salt dissolved into the water, and slowly she melted away. Miners did not think to move the statue, for why would they? Wherever they moved her she would still cry. The burden of the world would follow her wherever she might go. You see, they thought it was not her location in the mine that made her weep, it was her position in a terrible world that made her weep. A position separated from place, but position nonetheless.

Miners began to leave the mine, never to return. They said they could not work in such a place. They abandoned their stations. The food of Wieliczka grew bland and tasteless. They had banished all pleasure from their mouths to save the world Madonna wept for. A place of miracles and a place haunted by terrors of the world is what the mine became. The salt mine drew quiet. The clang of pick axes and shovels ceased. Madonna dissolved, lay abandoned on the mine floor by those who were at once pious to her. This is the story of the salt mine of Wieliczka."

Elli stopped and pinched another handful of orange mushrooms into her satchel. We walked a bit further and I watched the dog dig frantically, then move a few paces ahead, sniff the ground, and begin again.

"Do you believe such a story?" Elli asked.

"I'm not sure. I'm not sure if it's possible."

Elli nodded and added, "But you do believe such stories as this? Impossible made probable?"

I had no intention of clarifying my point. It was true, I did not understand the story nor did I think I needed to. It was also true I believe stories as wild as the salt mines of Wieliczka.

Elli continued. "A group was ordered to study the miracle. Priests, Cardinals, mine officials. Scientists. Best of their field soon flooded into the abandoned mine. And do you know what they found?

"That spring had been rainy. It had rained for weeks. Rivers had swollen, fields were soggy. In all of that rain, in all of that water it had moved toward the centre of the earth and one small path had led it to an opening right above Madonna's head. For overhead, above Madonna, water dripped in small, clear drops. Tears not of Madonna but of earth itself and they fell perfectly onto her face, and rolled down her cheek and began to dissolve the miner's faith. Now miners would have had to simply look up, toward the roof, toward where their holy and divine father lives to have seen water dripping. They could have saved Madonna by diverting the water's flow. But their eyes remained fixed on her form, resigned to God's will. There was nothing, they told themselves, to be done."

We stopped and rested on an outcropping of red rocks, speckled granite cleaved and split in tight lines and faults, like an orange slit open by the nature of its slices. We looked over Lake Ladoga. A few boats in the distance threw a small white wake. An airplane added its cloud to the high thin puffs that had been there all day. Elli pulled some tough, dried meat from her satchel and handed a small piece to the dog who took it gently from her hand and wandered a few feet away and began to chew it. She handed me a small piece.

"Which story to believe? If you are a pious person perhaps the first story. Miracles happen every day, don't they? And all around us. Perhaps miracles are so frequent that we count them as we would any other thing, part of the order of the universe. An atom splitting is not theory but divinity, you could say.

"Or, if you are a person of reason, of order and science, then what we call miracles are simply matters of science, not random tosses of God's dice but modelled order of the cosmos, bones of the universe that always grow in the same order and work together in skeletons.

"But there is the third person type, a person not concerned with miracle nor geology of situation, only outcome. You see, in the end, Madonna still vanished. In the end, faith and reason aside, it was all Kaputt. It had all gone to pieces."

Elli said nothing more but rose a few minutes later after we had cleared a great silence between us. She leaned against a rock and pushed herself up.

"Let's move back. It will rain soon."

Elli spoke with confidence. There was not a cloud in the sky but I believed her, or at least believed in the premise. "You know," she said, "people say that this lake too has performed a miracle, though wholly evil in its doing."

I found Elli's eyes and I saw for the first time how deep they were, how endless they moved about in her head, how much they saw of this world, as if so old they were ageless.

The Reindeer

It did not rain that day nor that night. It did not rain again that entire summer. The sun baked the wilderness and the trees grew brittle, the ground grew hollow. Each step echoed deep into the soil now empty of its water. It was late August and the night sky had returned, the brightest stars returning first, then night by night, the darkness acting as a cosmic sieve sorting the faintest stars back into the night.

That summer my life began to disappear into something unbounded. I learned to forage for mushrooms like Elli did. I walked the forest for hours, through the white birch and red granite. I learned to read it. The green sun filtered through the quaking leaves and all around was the allusion of water, though none existed but in the great lake always hovering on the horizon. Then the trees grew light and the leaves fell and the lake still beat against the rocky shore. The dog began to follow me through the woods. I had never heard Elli say its name and I never asked. I tried several names on it, boring variations of common ones but she responded to nothing. The only thing that she would return to was a loud sharp whistle.

I learned a few words of Elli's mother tongue, Swedish, a few of her adopted one, Russian. We saw no one most days accept each other. We spent the summer and fall in near isolation in the wilderness. Once every other week, Elli walked to a town some distance away to barter for simple things: grains and coffee and teas, though mostly we ate what we found or salvaged or stole. We were border dwellers. We lived in a place on the border between two states: Finland and Russia, the modern world and the old one.

Occasionally I would charge my phone and check for messages. A few friends with simple messages checking in, the chain of correspondences always ending with a series of question marks. To squelch any perceived panic I simply responded "out of town" and turned off the phone.

There were several messages from the hospital. I recognized the number. I deleted them before listening to them. I knew enough of what they said. Either my father was alive, which I knew he was not, or it was a request that his things, his body, be dealt with. I imagined him driftless now in the afterworld, a soul without a perch, and in the physical world, an unclaimed body among the lockers of the morgue. I did not feel sorry for him even though I tried. He had lived his life as if it were dictated, as if it could not be altered. I thought of him telling yet another story as invincible as history itself, about the time he spent the afterlife in an icebox, unclaimed and unwanted.

C recovered slowly. The doctor managed to set his bone but there was little we could do for his pain. The aspirin didn't work. The herbal remedies did nothing. He slept and woke in feverish dreams. He was sick, his body fighting some unseen battles. I brought him food, mostly soups made from lichens and mushrooms, which he ate silently, speaking only enough to state his dissatisfaction and to ask for salt. He did not seem upset with me for the accident, or he did not remember the event. He may not have even recalled the fall. A few times I wondered if it would come back to him and I would sit near his bed at night, thinking briefly about ending that chance for him. But I did nothing. I kept bringing salt.

In the forest I became familiar with the sounds. The clearest were the church bells, the motorboats, the gunshots. I had to reorient myself to the sounds the humans did not create — the squirrels, the crows, the wolves. The rustle of the leaves before a wind, the rustle of the leaves after one.

Throughout the forest the calls of cuckoos echoed. When I heard their call, I would look up and find the stripped underbelly of the birds, flitting from nest to nest. I became enthralled with the parasitizing of the birds, how they would lay their eggs in other nests, having not the responsibility nor the burden of raising brood, yet knowing they would somehow live on in another.

While foraging I would occasionally find a small fledgling dead on the forest floor, a near naked chick with its beak the size of its entire head. I knew the cuckoo chick had forced the other bird from the nest, out competing it with its rapid growth. Outsizing it. Outsmarting it. But the forest had changed me. The wilderness and the edge of living in it, surviving off it, had changed me. I did not feel sorry for this hatchling. I found it pathetic. Why should the cuckoo not win? Why should its ability to think a step ahead of every other bird not be rewarded? As I walked through the woods I would mimic the bird, forcing with a heavy breath its call out of my mouth — *goo-koo, goo-koo* — while the dog trotted beside me looking for small, ortolan meals on the forest floor.

A few times I had gone with Elli into the village to barter for supplies. I had wrapped myself in a babushka and remained quiet, standing a few feet from Elli as she spoke in Russian to the vendors, buying grain and eggs and coffee. Occasionally she would gesture in my direction and I would pick up the word for "niece" and with that she would explain away my presence and return to the negotiations. Though she had some money, she often bartered the wild forages we collected — the berries, the mushrooms — for the things she needed. I became enthralled with her way of life, how she moved in the world indifferent to its being and with little regard for its, or her, continuation.

We began to expand our walks, up and down the coast searching for thin-wired fences. Behind these fences were cattle and goats and often horses. We took notes of every paddock, every field, the number of horses, and marked in our minds the fence lines. We timed our trips along the coast. At night I walked the paths alone, counting my footfalls.

As the days grew shorter, I grew restless. I spent nights by the shore, lost in the reflection of the stars off the lake's smooth glass surface. Every dead black corner of the universe, every star that could send its light met here, in this lake near the end of the world and then reflecting off the lake into my eye. I swallowed the universe in a blink. Even in the coming chill of the nights I would slip into the water, black and still. It was deep and cool and pockets of cold mixed below me as I floated on my back and surrendered wholly to the night. I gave myself over to the possibility of becoming some creature of the deep. I swam deeper and deeper. I filled my ears with the prenatal rush and whorl of water, it dampened the world on the outside and returned me to the place before all places, before the time of men and horses and war and life and death. In these moments I could not find the grace. The peace that comes is the growing static of chaos, of sparks leaping from state to state. I could not find it. I slept to nothing. I woke to less.

It was mid-autumn. The birch were yellow. We bartered for grain and eggs and we walked with Petra, one of Elli's few friends. The dog followed closely. It sniffed at the bag of barley and Elli smacked it on its head. "*Nyet, nyet!*" she yelled and the dog shied and trotted a few paces behind us.

We walked along the street north of town to a small cluster of thatched roof houses that in my mind no longer existed in this world, an archaic reminder from a world years ago, to Petra's home.

"I have never seen these roofs before," I said and pointed to the sheaves of straw above the entrance.

"Yes, yes," said Petra. "We must at least look it. It just hides modern inside," And she smiled at me. I looked up again and saw the black tarry surface of a roof beneath the sheaves.

The house was small and dark and I could smell the burning damp wood. An orange cat moved from the stack of wooden crates into a recess in the wall and disappeared.

"Sit, I make food for us to eat now." And Elli and I sat in the living room. The dog remained outside and I heard her soft whimpers through the door.

Through the only window in the house, I watched over the distant fields to the east. I saw airplanes pass through the sky, in the fading daylight their red and green lights becoming artificial stars.

Petra brought us some tea and bread. It was the same bitter tea we drank all summer and fall, and warm dense bread with sour smelling butter. She set the food on the small table between the several chairs in the room.

"So you know my niece is here because of the lake, Petra?"

Petra dipped a ladle into a large pot and smelled it, then sipped it. The house smelled of onions. She looked at us from the kitchen.

"She is not your niece, Elli. Why family story?"

"Because we are all family, Petra!"

They exchanged a few words in Russian and Petra placed the lid back on the pot. She walked back into the room and sat in a caned chair. The rushes were thin and needed replacing. A few had torn and split and hung touching the ground.

"So she seeks salt mine!" Petra joked.

We sipped the tea and Petra and Elli talked half in Russian, half in English. As they gossiped I fixed my gaze on the hole where the orange cat disappeared and waited for its return.

We let a silence fall over us and an unmuffled car rumbled by, the sound from its cracked muffler resonated in the house.

"So you came for miracles but you have been warned by Elli, so you still stay for miracles then? Hmm?" Petra said.

Elli nodded in slow agreement.

"I'm not sure what to say. I had not thought of it as a miracle."

"Yes, but Curzi, it is true, miracle you seek." Petra looked deep into my face and I felt panicked by her words.

Petra threw up her hands. "Ah ha!" she cried. "There is no miracle in a place like this. We only believe in rotten. Everything is for sale and if you don't believe that you are lying. And if you agree you are probably being paid to say so!"

They laughed, and Elli added, "Yes, it is all rotten. Like an apple on the ground too long."

"Did you know that apple seed does not grow the true tree they fall from?" Petra asked me.

"No, I didn't know."

"Yes, you must cut them, take a small piece of living thing from itself if you want the same fruit."

Outside the sky was stacked in coloured layers. The horizon rose in red to orange to yellow and faded overhead into blue and purple.

"My father was in the war you know," Petra said. "I know why you are here. Elli has told me. Would it spoil the story if I tell you what he saw?"

I look to Elli but she only looked at her tea, then she closed her eyes and leaned her head back against the chair.

"Well, if you do not have an answer I'll give you one," she said.

"Before the new country, before the revolution, my grandfather lived in a distant country, a long way from here. He was a poor farmhand and he would rise in the morning before light and drink his tea and walk many miles to the field where he worked. Now my grandfather was large and a good worker. His hands were twice the size of other field hands and his scythe was sharper than any other in all of the country. He could take an acre of barley in one day when other men took half that. He would pass everyday, a house with the old farmer who could no longer swing his scythe for he was too frail and old. So the farmer's daughter worked as a housemaid in the village for money. After long days in the field he would walk back to his house and he would pass the old farmer's house and he would pass the farmer's daughter hanging linens outside.

"My grandfather would tip his hat in courtesy to the daughter as he passed but he would not get a reply. He did this for many months and for many years. Every day he would walk after his tea, long dark road to his fields and then long road home and everyday he would tip his cap to the farmer's daughter.

"One day, the longest of the year, my grandfather again walked past the old farmer's house and tipped his cap to the daughter who hung linen on the lines. When he did not get a response from the daughter he walked to her and greeted the daughter.

'How do you do ma'am?' my grandfather asked.

'Why, quite well, thank you sir.'

'May I speak with your father?' my grandfather asked and the daughter went into the house and fetched her father.

'Sir, if I may ask, I pass your house every day on my way to the farm and every day I tip my hat to your daughter but she does not reply. I would like to state that I would much like to know if I may get your blessing so that she might reply in kind as I pass your house.

"The farmer looked over my grandfather, then looked over his daughter who now stood in the corner of the porch with her head hung low.

'You say that every day you pass you tip your hat to my daughter?'

'Yes sir.'

'And that every day you receive no reply?'

'That is true sir.'

'And in your passing what is it that you call out to her?'

'I beg your pardon?'

'What is it that you greet her with that you do not get a response?'

'Why I only greet her with a tip of my cap.'

'I see, and how is it then that you tell a story?'

'I'm sorry, I do not understand.'

'If you do not speak then I do not understand how it is that you tell a story?'

My grandfather did not have an answer. He looked at the old farmer confused.

The farmer asked his daughter to raise her head and she did and she stared at my grandfather with eyes that passed through him, dulled in evening light.

'Do you see my daughter's eyes? They are made of glass. She cannot see.'

My grandfather again looked at the farmer's daughter and could see her eyes were made of glass.

'So you see, I ask how it is you tell a story to those who do not have eyes to see it for themselves?'"

Petra rested and leaned back and took a long sip of tea. Elli nodded and I felt lost in this world, lost in the tales of this old place. I had found my father once again as a story, a place, an idea that should be spoken in some way other than a riddle.

"So you see now, Curzi. That daughter was my grandmother."

"No, I don't see it. I don't understand why we all speak in parables and riddles. Why is that woman your grandmother? Why?"

Both Petra and Elli laughed. I turned and looked out the window again and watched as the last light of day slipped away.

"Because he told her his story."

The rest of that summer the arctic boiled and Siberia baked. I saw in newspapers pictures of helicopters dropping red liquid on fires. The north of the country, of the world, was burning. Giant holes opened into the permafrost, swallowing everything that once covered the surface. They swallowed everything. I understood how easy it was for us to push something aside, to stare into the eyes of the Madonna and ask her why she weeps, to weep with her instead of turning to look for an answer beyond a miracle. I understood why we must tell stories to those with glass eyes.

Late in the fall, a few weeks before the conflagration, the dog and I went alone to the village to buy some coffee and grain. I took with me a satchel of dried mushrooms to barter. I visited one of the few women I knew, but she spoke only Russian. Few of these poor peasants spoke English, but we did our exchange prearranged with Elli's help.

As I bartered the dried goods, I caught the eye of two policemen walking through the square. They stopped and spoke quickly to each other. I had never seen them before and I watched as they cut their way through the crowd. They kept their thumbs in their glossy black belt. I could see a baton and several pistols fastened to their hips. One of the men locked eyes on me and I turned quickly back to the old woman weighing the dried mushrooms. I pulled my scarf up higher onto my head and shrunk my shoulders lower, and looked away. The dog milled slowly at my feet. I felt my cheeks flush and my fingers turn numb. I contemplated running, gaining a head start but my feet were frozen into the ground. My feet were lead pigs. The old lady counted slowly, scooping slow cups of mushrooms from one container to another.

"Good evening." One of the police stood to my side. I could sense the other was a few feet behind me.

"It's a lovely evening, no?"

I did not understand him, I caught the word for night but I nodded in agreement.

He looked past my shoulder to the police standing behind me.

"Do you have ID?" he asked.

I feigned that I did not understand.

"ID?" and he put his fingers together for the shape of a card. He said something quick and sharp to the other officer behind me and I set my bag on the ground and began to rifle though it, not knowing what it was I was going to hand them. I did not have an ID and even if I had my American passport, it was not something I would hand over. The dog approached the questioning officer and began a low growl, its hackles starting to rise. The police officer said something in the tone of "nice dog" in Russian and lifted a hand to his waist and began to unclip his pistol when the dog leaped and bit his thigh. The police officer fell back and began screaming and the other officer rushed past me, bumping me into the lady's table. Her display tipped over and she shouted. My heart raced. I took a large piece of wood from the shelves she had arranged and swung it, striking the second officer square in the ear. Blood began to spill from his temple and he fell sideways, catching the corner of the old lady's table. The dog was still latched onto the other officer's leg and blood was now darkening his light blue pants.

The crowd had swelled around the scene and villagers who had been in shops spilled into the streets. I ran for the woods. I passed two young men in jumpsuits wiping grease off their hands. They pointed at me, laughing. "Thief, thief!" they yelled.

My heart was pumping so fast I felt I might pass out but I kept running. I could not bring myself to turn and look back. I was worried I would see a chasing mob, several police officers with pistols pointed squarely at my head. I neared the forest's edge. I heard two sharp reports and covered my head as I fell to the ground. I began to crawl until I found my footing and then I ran. I could hear the villagers scream as I disappeared into the wilderness. I sprinted until I reached the korsu at the edge of the lake. When I finally turned back there was no one.

Elli took my warning and we left the korsu and moved things around the forest to conceal our location. We leaned dead fall against our door. We leafed over our paths. The chimney pipe was dismantled. We ate cold soaked oats for days. At night we heard a distant circling of a helicopter and the voices of men shouting in the woods. We could not leave. I dreamed in the night of the police officer's face, his severe brow, his nose pinched in the middle, flattened from some past blow. The deep pockmarks that line his cheeks, the heavy breath of men of war. I dreamt it all was melting, his face on fire laughing as I swam into the lake, but the lake had gone, evaporated into the endless heat.

It had been three days since we heard the helicopters and the men calling in the woods, when we opened the door to an empty forest and the dog was waiting, shivering and hungry. I fell and wrapped my arms around her. It sat whimpering and shivering. Elli pulled a gristly cut of meat from a tin and tossed it to the ground and the dog freed itself and began to gnaw with the side of its mouth.

We began to walk the forest again, looking for tracks of the police but we found little. A few boot prints in some dusty soil but nothing else.

"They will not stop," Elli said. "These men have nothing but time. We will be hunted. This place is rotten."

I was quiet. I could not but feel I had brought this on us somehow beside coincidence. I followed a few paces off from Elli.

"This may be true." Elli stopped and looked at me, agreeing with herself. "But soon there will be nothing left to hunt." And with this she kept walking and we traced the lake once more.

The next day the sky sank into a gunmetal grey. Heavy, sagging clouds mimicked the rolling hills under them and moved quickly flowing south. It was mid-October and the reign of cold from the arctic was early and it settled heavy over us. We kept a near constant fire but we still could not keep warm. The cold was too deep. The earth flashed frozen, any leaf still left attached to the trees turned to brittle paper and shattered on the ground. The wind turned over the lake and beat against the rocky shore and ice built layer after layer on the granite. The hollowed, empty earth was locked in an instant ice age.

On our last night we huddled against the wood stove. The fire warmed our fingers but little else. The wind found its way through every crack in the korsu and stung like nettles the skin left exposed for it to touch.

C, in the back bedroom, lay as he had for months now. His bedsores had grown worse and though I bathed him I resented him. We had layered him with blankets of down and wool. His weak body could barely turn. The days were shrinking, the nights growing longer. Elli and I would soon leave and walk the paths we had traced for months to make real what we could, to tell our story.

The Flies

I entered C's room quietly and I sat next to his bed. His head was turned to the wall and I felt his eyes open and stare past the chinking in the logs.

"C," I said, "we have to go. Elli and I are leaving tonight." My words were hollow and empty. I could feel them reach nothing. I knew C would not leave. He did not want to. He did not need to.

For a minute, we talked to each other in our minds, each saying what the other would not, could not. My own brother, once so much older, wiser in my eyes now my charge, my patient. A patient I had created. I broke the silence.

"C, do you remember, we were — you were — what, thirteen and I was nine, I think, and that blizzard? We woke up and it was snowing so hard it was like rain. Big white rain drops. And cold. The wind. Do you remember? The snow was piling up on our door and we kept opening it to see how much higher it had become. Then dad told us to get dressed. We put on our snow clothes. Do you remember how upset mom was? She begged him not to leave. Not to go out into the storm but he wouldn't listen. Do you remember?

"I was in the back entry, putting my boots on and he hit her C. I could see it from the back room by the back door. I watched them in the kitchen. He hit her across the face and told her that it was not her place to tell him what to do with his children. It was the first time I saw him hit her, and I froze. I couldn't move. Mom just sat at the kitchen table and didn't say a word. She didn't even touch her face. Just sat down and lit a cigarette and looked out the window near the sink. I couldn't move. I felt so — so connected to her in some way. Then dad walked back to me, he snapped at me, 'Get them on!' and I fell out of my trance.

"Do you remember how cold and miserable that walk to the lake was? Do you remember dad thinking we could take the Buick. We rocked back and forth in that spot for what seemed like hours, dad cursing each time the wheels spun. I know he had to see it, but why drag us? Why slow himself down with us?

"God, that walk was cold. I wanted to cry but I was so worried my eyes would freeze shut if I did. We just kept moving and he kept telling us not to stop. He said this is what it was like, it was the perfect conditions, that everything that was true then was true now.

"When we reached the lake, the wind. Jesus the wind was terrible. I couldn't open my eyes. Do you remember the sound the lake made? It was screaming. It was a high-pitched squeal, just like the slaughterhouse. It was that same squeal I heard muffled through the walls every time I went to work with dad. It would not stop and I could not unhear it. It was the ice. The shore had frozen so quickly huge slabs of ice were piling over one another as the wind pushed them onto the shore. I knew dad heard it too. We all heard it. I don't know if he was just immune to the sounds of death by then or if he had somehow become even more in tune with it, reading each cry for help in its own unique way. I don't know how he heard it, but I know he heard it.

"I think I know what dad wanted to see that day. He wanted to see the lake freeze over solid. He wanted it to be true. He had to see the transformation. Otherwise, what? Otherwise, his story was a lie? His life was a lie? I don't know. I really do think he thought the whole goddamn lake would be frozen solid. I really think that. You tell yourself something long enough and you are bound to believe it at some point. If we never believe the things we tell ourselves over and over then those things will eat away at us, like water to ice, until we just shatter, break apart, melt into something else.

"I know what I saw. Do you remember it, C? It wasn't frozen. The lake was churning behind the screaming ice. And for years I thought this is what dad saw too. But I'm not so sure anymore.

"Back then I never thought I'd be on this side of it, you know, the end. I never could think of a time when I would be closer to the end than the beginning. It is so much easier to contemplate the start. It's an event, a time, a place. But death? What is that? It's some abstract state. I don't know where, but it is not here, it wasn't there. Some in-between place. I don't think dad had thought once about his death, not once before that day at the shore with the wind choking us and the spray of the lake coating our jackets. I think he — and I think this too — thought that there is some idea, some thing we bury in our head as the absolute truth, the magnetic north of our life and we follow it, guided toward it. Maybe money or fame, or shit like that, or maybe a stupid story about a lake flashing frozen and swallowing some horses. Maybe we don't get to choose what becomes our absolute truth. Maybe it chooses us.

"I remember walking back and dad mentioning something about the winds, or the weather, some barometric anomaly that kept the lake from freezing over. He just couldn't believe the lake wouldn't freeze. It was the only moment of his life I think he ever regretted.

"I was so cold when we got home, I swear I caught a fever. A fever worse than in Helsinki. Mom made us soup and put us right to bed. It was still light out. Snow still falling. It was a break in the blizzard. I don't know if there are eyes in blizzards like in hurricanes but the wind nearly stopped, the heavy wet snow stopped. I watched a new snowfall. It looked like it was air itself. It was the snow that sparkles. It was so light and it fell so peacefully. I remember sitting in bed watching it fall for hours. I couldn't move. It was the most beautiful thing I had ever seen. The snow floated so slowly I could watch each flake dance in the still air. I thought — I thought, this is what heaven is like. This is what happens when you die. Snow falls all around you, each flake so overwhelmingly beautiful you can only cry at the beauty. I laid next to the window and I cried."

C didn't move. He didn't turn his head. I listened for something, for anything, but I heard nothing. Only the soft rise and fall of his breath. I could smell the wood stove drafting in the cold.

"I'm sorry, C. I should never have come to see you. I never should have come to see dad. But now." I stopped.

What was now? What did I know in this moment, weeks removed from the warmth of southern California, from a life I had known so well as my own? And now, lost in some Russian forest with old age herself and a dog, about to walk a path which can only be travelled in one direction. I wanted to see snow fall again.

I stood and said goodbye to C. I thought he might rise too. I thought he would not resign himself to the end in this way. But he didn't. I cannot say he could have. He may have wanted too but I had given him a choice when there was nothing left to choose.

C spoke up.

"Do you know how it ends?"

I paused. "How what ends?"

"The book. Do you know how it ends?" I thought for a moment and then I remember the book, my namesake's book I had bought and neglected since we arrived in the Russian forest.

C turned toward me and adjusted his body, slowly, grimacing as he turned. His face was tight and loose at the same time. He looked aged, ashen. He looked like our old house, back in Chicago. He looked like everything around us. The patina of his face of white stubble and deep-set wrinkles looked much like the shallow fjords cut into Lake Ladoga.

"Sit. Sit a minute more."

I sat and the C began in a low voice. He was hoarse.

"Curzio goes back to Naples, to find his home after the war, after prison. He's thinking of the good things, the sea and the food and the gentle clean breezes. But do you know what he finds? Ruins. Bodies. Dead bodies lying in the streets. He cries at the sight of the sea but not at the stacks and scores of the bodies. He had been all over Europe, seen death, disease, the macabre, the infamous. He had dined on the best food, drank the best wine with the worst people, but to him, it was all out there, away from his home. It was never supposed to be part of him. He always thought he could leave it. But at the end of the book he sees it in his home. He sees it as part of him too. But do you know how the book really ends?"

I realized C had read the book, read it completely, but never once had mentioned it to me. The book that made our father our father, the story that became him in all our own imagined worlds. I had not read it. I had not read the book because I did not want to get closer to my father, to understand any more than I had to about our father. That book, the stories it held would be like a map of all I did not know about that man and I wanted some large part of that road to remain dark, shrouded in night. But C had read it. C had exposed the night to the day and found the very fault lines that ran through our house and he filled them in with sand, repetitively, constantly, watching it sieve its way through the cracks and continue deep into the crevasses until every trace of a fissure was gone. It was a Sisyphean task, relentless, thankless. But he did it. He did it because, for him, it removed the shell around our father, it laid bare his anatomy, his flesh and bones.

C continued. "Curzio wants a drink of water and he stops at a small store and an old man is sitting there and he asks for a glass of water. There are flies everywhere, they are coating his mouth, the old man's face, they cover the bodies in the sea, in the rubble. They line the walls. He has come all this way, back to what he thought was home but the flies, they had won. They were everywhere. He couldn't escape them.

"The myth of the horses and the frozen lake, this is where dad stopped. He failed to believe, to see what was next. But Curzi, even if the myth is true, even if this universe-defining thing can happen, in the end the horses will rot. Every event, every moment, every instance born in truth or lie decays and the flies will always find it."

C finished and closed his eyes. There was little more to say.

"Goodbye C." He said nothing, then coughed. I handed him a glass of water. He drank it slowly and I stood to leave. As I left, his breath turned shallow and light like a small breeze blowing against an icy shore.

This is what will happen next.

Elli and I will leave the korsu and its cold. With my first breath I will seize.

"Breathe," she will say. "Take the tea." And she will hand me the bark tea and I will swallow it.

We will follow the paths we have spent all summer cutting in the forest and we will move quickly. The dog will follow close and run a few paces ahead and stop, turn its ears, point them in the dark to a distant noise that I cannot hear. I will watch her head and wait for her movement but she will drop the sound and we will move again. We will stop at a fork. Elli will hand me a heavy pair of bolt cutters. When I take them, I will feel the fingers of her hand, their rough skin brushing against mine. She will have removed her mittens.

"Your hands," I will say, but I will stop. I will remove my mittens and she will grip my bare hands. I will feel in her hand the landscape of this place, the lost trees, the sharply cut boulders. I will feel age in her hands but I will be lost in the idea, the threat of it. Moving, living, pushing toward that ending arrests a person with such fear there cannot ever be time to wrestle it to a knee, to make peace with it.

Elli will not say anything. She will turn and begin her walk south along the shore and I will watch her figure through the small trees skirting the path as she disappears. She will walk lightly on her toes and her heels will touch the earth only for a moment before she floats away. The dog will pause and look between us. I will shoo it toward Elli but it will not move. It will let out a small whimper then it will turn and walk the path with Elli. We are all already afraid of becoming moored.

I will cut through the spruce to the north and walk for an hour and then another. Soon my core will have warmed, my feet and hands and my own heat will move me forward. The moon will rise yellow over the southern shore of the lake and its pockmarks will reflect on the rippling surface. I will cut every fence I see. My cutters will pinch tight the wire until it snaps in tension, springs like reverb echoing through the trees. A few cattle will stir as I move.

I will sweep across the land and free it of all artificial boundaries. Soon I will no longer walk, I will be water lapping over rocks and I will not speak and I will not whisper and I will not question the way I am and what I have become.

A bright green ribbon will sweep over the sky and move in the shape of a Möbius strip and I will pause and wait for something to fall from it, to brush against me, but nothing will. Each small atom will pick an arc across the sky and follow it, lighting a path and then burning to completion before the horizon. My warm breath will fog the night and then freeze in the air, turn to crystals before falling back to the frozen parched earth.

With each fence line I snap I will drive the horses away from the lake. They will not see me approach in the night, but my hand, as soon as it touches their greasy coat, will send them flitting through the fields. Under the rising moon I will watch them group and move as if their every motion was dictated not by the evolution of living things but by the physics of the inanimate, the rules of waves and seas. They will move along the worn paths where boundaries once were, the places they have worn thin with their wide flat feet until they realize that the boundary is no longer there, the fences gone, and they will cut to new earth in terror and in pride, both free and constrained by what will be. I will send every horse deeper into the wilderness, further from the lake.

I will think of Cortez and his nineteen horses, what they saw that first time they touched down on that foreign soil. From those nineteen horses, he brought a new breed of conquest. A new breed of war. So foreign was that world to them they could not imagine how to ride its back, ride above it, on the backs of beasts. We hover over the world's rocky slopes and marshy flats, seeing but never touching. This is how we ride the world. The horse becomes our hands. Its hooves, our fingers. We let the ringing world vibrate through them as our way of knowing.

I will reach the far end of the path we have spent the better part of the summer carving through the wilderness and I will stop where its cleared width disappears into a heavy-branched woods. I will listen to the wind beat against the surface of the lake and I will listen for the clamber of hooves, but I will hear nothing. I will listen for the bark of the dog.

I will hear a loud pop, a sharp snap from behind me, from the trail I have taken and I will turn quickly and a black mass will take up my vision. I will feel the moist, sharp breath of its exhale on my face. I will reach out and touch its long snout and we will exchange the touch, both finding the other's anatomy.

The moon and the green ribbon above will light its black eyes. I will search but I will find nothing. Its black mane, greasy, the odour of rotting earth will leave me uneasy. I will hate every damn place they have touched, trotted over. I will feel the evil of their role and, in that moment, I will want nothing more than to become a butcher. Why, in those large eyes, will there be no reflection? No end? Why will I find nothing that comforts me in the beast of war, of carnage, of lost hope.

I will slap its withers and it will shy and I will hit it again and it will trot away, disappearing in the dark.

Across the lake I will see the orange glow of flames. Elli will have started. I will collect a small pile of tinder, shelter it against the wind and will strike a match above it. It will take instantly and I will fan it until I can no longer control what it is. It will consume the forest floor and the pile of loose branches and it will begin its assent, breathing in the cold wind as it climbs the trees. I will feel the hot air and my face will become blistered. It will sting and prick as it takes back the blood the cold has forced away. I will want to stay with it, be consumed by its warmth, but I have made my choice. It is ice.

I will begin back down the path and the flames will grow and follow. I will see bright white spots of light in the forest. The village will awaken. Their frantic movement of spotlights will signal running. It will be the frightened waves of the end. Voices will rise in the distance. Foreign shouts. Foreign screams. As if the tips of my fingers are made to drip flames, I will ignite every piece of dry tinder I find. The flames will consume everything. There will no longer be the green ribbons, the thousands of stars, the yellow moon of the night. It will all be consumed, burnt over. So greedy are the flames they will take my sight and I will see only it and what it can do. The villagers will flee, the horses will flee, both away from the lake, away from the water.

I will return to the point from where we started. Elli will be beside me. The fire will consume everything beyond us and we will stand on a cliff above the lake and above us the stars will fade to a colour beyond black that cannot be described or seen and we will wait for it, some burst or scream from the heavens but it will not come because the end will not be heard.

So, does it take only a seed, a nucleus, some mote of dust to begin something anew and wholly consuming?

Is that what I have become?

What was your last dream? It was not the sight of horses escaping flames, fleeing in heavy breath to the sea. This was not your last dream. It would have been too good. I won't let you have it. The peace that comes with knowing the story you have told is the truest life you could have lived. I will not let you so easily choose a path that ends in legend, that builds around you like ice forms on a windy lake against the shore, something so beautiful and polished no one can see to the fractured rock below.

This you do not get.

You get this instead.

A dry place. A mountain. A sun that does not set. It is a place you wander in, seeking but you do not find. Every direction is a rise, then another; sand dunes ripple like waves and shift in a scale of time you cannot witness because you are here forever. You climb the sand but your feet sink quickly and the sun heats the sand and it burns and stings against your bare feet. Each dune a different wave, but each dune the same. It is the same as the sea. Ever changing but remaining the same. You make it over one dune, but behind you the thing you wish to escape is still there. That parched mountain. Its cleaved faces. Its precipice you will never climb. You are thirsty. You must drink. But what can you drink? The sand moves like water but it is not water. You know this. How can you make it into something you cannot?

Each night you sleep the desert turns cold and you shiver. And each day you wake again at the foot of the mountain and you look out over the same golden sand, the same movement it has always been, and you burn. When will you climb the mountain? When will you turn to see what is atop it and not walk endlessly into the nothing beyond, into the same sky, the same earth, the same life you have always wanted but never had.

No.

This is your dream.

You climb the mountain but its edges are sharp and they cut clean lines in your hands but you do not bleed. Your fingers, your hands, become filled with deep cracks and they only grow deeper until you cannot see into them but you know that somewhere deep inside there is a bone and it can be broken. You climb. And soon you find the top. And on this top is a large cross. The same cross that hung above your bed. The same cross we turned to on Sundays. From this cross hangs not what you know but what you don't, hangs from it the body of a horse, splayed and stretched. And beside the cross is the executioner and he holds a hammer and a nail. He is ready to drive home the final pin, cleave the last solid hoof in half. The horse is drawing his head side to side, neighing. Then a crowd gathers and they weep. Are you crying also? Are you neighing? Look at it. Look at the horse and tell me you are not also one of the crowd weeping.

Do you want some answer to this dream? Do you want to wake to a wet place, an icy place? Do you want the heat or the cold? What is it you see now in that Golgotha? What will you give them? An empty womb? Dry beasts? You cannot look away and the horse bleeds. It neighs. It is too weak to scream. The executioner's hammer strikes the nail and the report of metal on metal sends a wail through the crowd and they weep. You weep too. Your eyes become the only thing in this place that is wet, that holds the form of the thing you have wanted for all these years. But this place, it is dry. It is not cold in this place and your tears, they evaporate from your face. They live not long enough to trace your cheeks. They surrender to the sky. Every tear in the crowd floats up and dissolves into the parched air. The water disappears. There is nothing left to freeze.

There is no ice in this place, and without the ice it cannot be held — the horses, your long soliloquies, your one and only story. Without ice there is no me, there is no us. There is nothing to hold that thin line between what you have spoken and what you have become. Isn't this, then, the last thing we will see? The last image we will have of a place before we leave it — something free, running wild between fire and ice, leaving rings in the sand along the shore.

ABOUT THE AUTHOR

Benjamin Fidler is a writer and carpenter.
He lives in Michigan